PUFFIN BOOKS

TEMPLE OF TERROR

The dark twisted power of the young Malbordus is reaching its zenith. The elves who raised him have set him one final task: to retrieve the five Dragon artefacts hidden for centuries in the lost city of Vatos, somewhere in the Desert of Skulls. Only when he has these in his grasp will he be able to rise up and engulf Allansia. Each day that passes brings him closer to them and only YOU can stop him!

YOUR mission is to cross the searing desert sands, find the mysterious lost city and destroy the treasures Malbordus seeks before he can reach them. But beware! Each step you take leads you closer to your doom . . .

Ian Livingstone, co-founder of the highly successful Games Workshop and editor of *White Dwarf*, has created a thrilling adventure of sword and sorcery, complete with an elaborate combat system and an adventure sheet to record your gains and losses. All you need is two dice, a pencil and an eraser.

Many dangers lie ahead and your success is by no means certain. It's up to YOU to decide which route to follow, which dangers to risk and which adversaries to fight!

Fighting Fantasy Gamebooks

Steve Jackson's SORCERY!

FIGHTING FANTASY – the Role-playing Game
THE RIDDLING REAVER
OUT OF THE PIT – Fighting Fantasy Monsters
TITAN – The Fighting Fantasy World

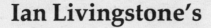

Ian Livingstone's

Temple of Terror

Illustrated by Bill Houston

Puffin Books

Puffin Books, Penguin Books Ltd, Harmondsworth, Middlesex, England
Viking Penguin Inc., 40 West 23rd Street, New York, New York 10010, U.S.A.
Penguin Books Australia Ltd, Ringwood, Victoria, Australia
Penguin Books Canada Ltd, 2801 John Street, Markham, Ontario, Canada L3R 1B4
Penguin Books (N.Z.) Ltd, 182–190 Wairau Road, Auckland 10, New Zealand

First published 1985
Reprinted 1985 (four times), 1986, 1987 (twice)

Printed and bound in Great Britain by
Cox & Wyman Ltd, Reading

Typeset in Linotron Palatino by
Rowland Phototypesetting Ltd,
Bury St Edmunds, Suffolk

CONTENTS

FIGHTING MONSTERS

Before embarking on your adventure, you must first determine your own strengths and weaknesses. You have in your possession a sword and a shield together with a rucksack containing Provisions (food and drink) for the trip.

You must use dice to determine your initial SKILL and STAMINA scores. On pages 20–21 there is an *Adventure Sheet* which you may use to record the details of an adventure. On it you will find boxes for recording your SKILL and STAMINA scores.

You are advised either to record your scores on the *Adventure Sheet* in pencil, or make photocopies of the page to use in future adventures.

Skill, Stamina and Luck

Roll one die. Add 6 to this number and enter this total in the SKILL box on the *Adventure Sheet*.

Roll both dice. Add 12 to the number rolled and enter this total in the STAMINA box.

There is also a LUCK box. Roll one die, add 6 to this number and enter this total in the LUCK box.

For reasons that will be explained below, SKILL, STAMINA and LUCK scores change constantly during an adventure. You must keep an accurate record of these scores and for this reason you are advised either to write small in the boxes or to keep an eraser handy. But never rub out your *Initial* scores. Although you may be awarded additional SKILL, STAMINA and LUCK points, these totals may never exceed your *Initial* scores, except on very rare occasions, when you will be instructed on a particular page.

Your SKILL score reflects your swordsmanship and general fighting expertise; the higher the better. Your STAMINA score reflects your general constitution, your will to survive, your determination and overall fitness; the higher your STAMINA score, the longer you will be able to survive. Your LUCK score indicates how naturally lucky a person you are. Luck – and magic – are facts of life in the fantasy kingdom you are about to explore.

Battles

You will often come across pages in the book which instruct you to fight a creature of some sort. An option to flee may be given, but if not – or if you choose to attack the creature anyway – you must resolve the battle as described below.

First record the creature's SKILL and STAMINA scores in the first vacant Monster Encounter Box on your *Adventure Sheet*. The scores for each creature are given in the book each time you have an encounter.

The sequence of combat is then:

1. Roll the two dice once for the creature. Add its SKILL score. This total is the creature's *Attack Strength*.
2. Roll the two dice once for yourself. Add the number rolled to your current SKILL score. This total is your *Attack Strength*.
3. If your *Attack Strength* is higher than that of the creature, you have wounded it. Proceed to step 4. If the creature's *Attack Strength* is higher than yours, it has wounded you. Proceed to step 5. If both *Attack Strength* totals are the same, you have avoided each other's blows – start the next *Attack Round* from step 1 above.
4. You have wounded the creature, so subtract 2 points from its STAMINA score. You may use your LUCK here to do additional damage (see over).

5. The creature has wounded you, so subtract 2 points from your own STAMINA score. Again you may use LUCK at this stage (see over).
6. Make the appropriate adjustments to either the creature's or your own STAMINA scores (and your LUCK score if you used LUCK – see over).
7. Begin the next *Attack Round* (repeat steps 1–6). This sequence continues until the STAMINA score of either you or the creature you are fighting has been reduced to zero (death).

Fighting More Than One Creature

If you come across more than one creature in a particular encounter, the instructions on that page will tell you how to handle the battle. Sometimes you will treat them as a single monster; sometimes you will fight each one in turn.

Luck

At various times during your adventure, either in battles or when you come across situations in which you could either be lucky or unlucky (details of these are given on the pages themselves), you may call on your luck to make the outcome more favourable. But beware! Using luck is a risky business and if you are *un*lucky, the results could be disastrous.

The procedure for using your luck is as follows: roll two dice. If the number rolled is *equal to or less than* your current LUCK score, you have been *lucky* and the result will go in your favour. If the number rolled is *higher* than your current LUCK score, you have been *unlucky* and you will be penalized.

This procedure is known as *Testing your Luck*. Each time you 'Test your Luck', you must subtract one point from your current LUCK score. Thus you will soon realize that the more you rely on your luck, the more risky this will become.

Using Luck in Battles

On certain pages of the book you will be told to *Test your Luck* and will be told the consequences of your being *lucky* or *unlucky*. However, in battles, you always have the *option* of using your luck either to inflict a more serious wound on a creature you have just wounded, or to minimize the effects of a wound the creature has just inflicted on you.

If you have just wounded the creature, you may *Test your Luck* as described above. If you are *lucky*, you have inflicted a severe wound and may subtract an *extra* 2 points from the creature's STAMINA score. However, if you are *unlucky*, the wound was a mere graze and you must restore 1 point to the creature's STAMINA (i.e. instead of scoring the normal 2 points of damage, you have now scored only 1).

If the creature has just wounded you, you may *Test your Luck* to try to minimize the wound. If you are *lucky*, you have managed to avoid the full damage of the blow. Restore 1 point of STAMINA (i.e. instead of doing 2 points of damage it has done only 1). If you are *unlucky*, you have taken a more serious blow. Subtract 1 *extra* STAMINA point.

Remember that you must subtract 1 point from your own LUCK score each time you *Test your Luck*.

Restoring Skill, Stamina and Luck

Skill

Your SKILL score will not change much during your adventure. Occasionally, a page may give instructions to increase or decrease your SKILL score. A Magic Weapon may increase your SKILL, but remember that only one weapon can be used at a time! You cannot claim 2 SKILL bonuses for carrying two Magic Swords. Your SKILL score can never exceed its *Initial* value unless specifically instructed.

Stamina and Provisions

Your STAMINA score will change a lot during your adventure as you fight monsters and undertake arduous tasks. As you near your goal, your STAMINA level may be dangerously low and battles may be particularly risky, so be careful!

Your backpack contains enough Provisions for ten meals. You may rest and eat at any time except when fighting, but you may eat only one meal at a time. Eating a meal restores 4 STAMINA points. When you eat a meal, add 4 points to your STAMINA score and deduct 1 point from your Provisions. A separate Provisions Remaining box is provided on the *Adventure Sheet* for recording details of Provisions. Remember that you have a long way to go, so use your Provisions wisely! Remember also that your STAMINA score may never exceed its *Initial* value unless specifically instructed on a page.

Luck

Additions to your LUCK score are awarded through the adventure when you have been particularly lucky. Details are given on the pages of the book. Remember that, as with SKILL and STAMINA, your LUCK score may never exceed its *Initial* value.

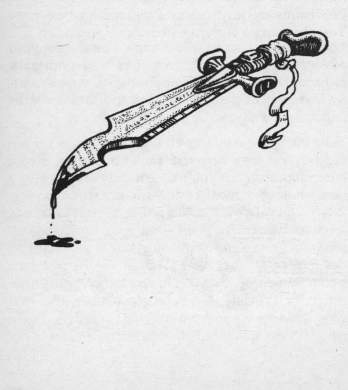

EQUIPMENT

You will start your adventure with a bare minimum of equipment, but you may find other items during your travels. You are armed with a sword and are dressed in leather armour. You have a rucksack (haversack, backpack) on your back to hold your Provisions and any treasures you may come across. You also carry a lantern which lights your way.

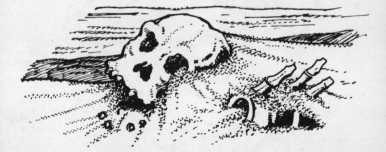

HINTS ON PLAY

Your journey will be perilous and you are likely to fail on your first attempt. Make notes and draw a map as you explore – this map will be invaluable in future adventures and enable you to progress rapidly through to unexplored sections.

Not all areas contain treasure; many merely contain traps and creatures which you will no doubt fall foul of. You may make wrong turnings during your quest and while you may indeed progress through to your ultimate destination, it is by no means certain that you will find what you are searching for.

It will be realized that entries make no sense if read in numerical order. It is essential that you read only the entries you are instructed to read. Reading other entries will only cause confusion and may lessen the excitement during play.

The one true way involves a minimum of risk and any player, no matter how weak on initial dice rolls, should be able to get through fairly easily.

May the luck of the gods go with you on the adventure ahead!

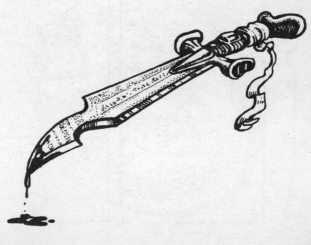

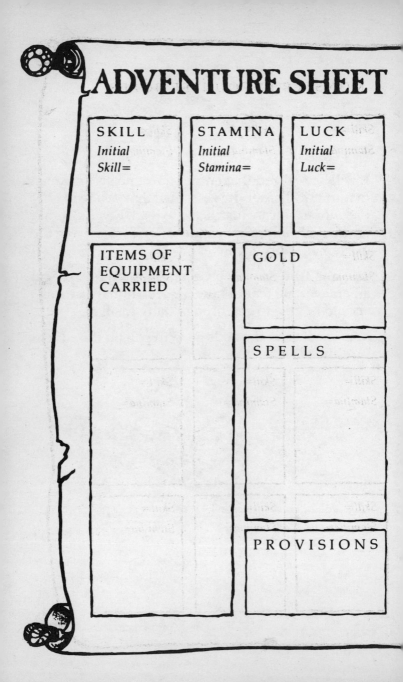

ADVENTURE SHEET

SKILL
Initial Skill=

STAMINA
Initial Stamina=

LUCK
Initial Luck=

ITEMS OF EQUIPMENT CARRIED

GOLD

SPELLS

PROVISIONS

MONSTER ENCOUNTER BOXES

Skill= *Stamina=*	*Skill=* *Stamina=*	*Skill=* *Stamina=*
Skill= *Stamina=*	*Skill=* *Stamina=*	*Skill=* *Stamina=*
Skill= *Stamina=*	*Skill=* *Stamina=*	*Skill=* *Stamina=*
Skill= *Stamina=*	*Skill=* *Stamina=*	*Skill=* *Stamina=*

BACKGROUND

Perhaps it was because he was born during a full moon, with wolves howling around his mother's forest hut, that Malbordus's nature was evil. Perhaps it was something more sinister than that. But it is certain that, after his mother abandoned him, Malbordus grew up in Darkwood Forest in the care of Darkside Elves. He was taught the Elves' wicked ways, and also discovered powers of his own. He could make plants wither and die simply by snapping his fingers; he could make animals obey him with his piercing gaze. The Elves urged him on and helped him develop his powers, so that they could teach him the arcane and evil magic of the ancient Elf Lords – magic so vile and powerful that it kills unworthy users. In pursuit of such evil powers, Malbordus grew into manhood. In order to prove to the Elves that he was ready to receive the Elf Lords' knowledge, he first had to pass a test. He was ordered to journey south to the Desert of Skulls to find the lost city of Vatos. In the city were hidden five Dragon artefacts which he would have to find and collect. A simple incantation would bring the Dragons to life to serve the forces of evil. Malbordus would then instruct them to fly him back to Darkwood Forest, where a massive army would be assembling. He would receive the ancient powers and lead the hordes of chaos across Allansia in an unstoppable wave of death and destruction.

It was only by a stroke of luck that these terrible plans were discovered. On the edge of Darkwood Forest lived a strange old Wizard named Yaztromo. Something of an eccentric, he lived alone in his tower, practising simple magic and communicating with animals and birds. He was always willing to sell small magic items, so that he could afford to have brought to him delicious cakes from all over Allansia. His sweet tooth was the cause of his only link with the outside world, as he rarely left his tower. It was therefore much to everyone's surprise that he came huffing and puffing into the village of Stonebridge. What could possibly have forced old Yaztromo to venture through Darkwood Forest to Stonebridge? All the Dwarfs who lived there were eager to find out, and a message was sent to Gillibran, their king.

After the rigours of a recent quest, you are resting in Stonebridge, enjoying the merry company of the Dwarfs. Your wounds are almost healed and the local blacksmith has honed the blade of your sword as only Dwarfs can. Resting on a porch with your feet up on the railing, you are intrigued by the commotion in front of you in the village square. Followed by a throng of inquisitive Dwarfs, Yaztromo climbs the stone steps of Gillibran's house and is warmly greeted at the top by the king. The crowd falls silent when Gillibran raises his hand, and Yaztromo turns to speak. You slide out of your chair and join the crowd to hear what the Wizard has to say. With a glum expression, his face almost as long as his beard, Yaztromo relates the bad news concerning Malbordus. The Dwarfs look up apprehensively as though expecting the five Dragons to descend upon them at any moment. He calls on them to show courage, saying, 'Friends, look on the bright side. At least we are warned of our impending doom, thanks to my pet crow who overheard the conversation between the Dark Elves and Malbordus. What we must do now is find somebody who can reach the lost city before Malbordus and destroy the Dragon artefacts. We need a fearless young warrior who is willing to risk life and limb to save us all. Is there one among you who would volunteer?'

Each Dwarf looks around to see if another has dared to accept the challenge. Standing there watching the worried Dwarfs, you realize that there is only one thing you can do. With a wry smile on your face, you raise your arm in the air and offer your services. Yaztromo sees you and says, 'Haven't I seen you somewhere before? Never mind, you look like the kind of person we want. Make way for our brave volunteer. We must leave for my tower immediately. Come along, let's be off. You have a lot to learn, but I cannot teach you much until we are safely through Darkwood Forest and inside my laboratory.'

You hardly have time to cram your belongings into your backpack before the impatient Wizard leads you out of Stonebridge towards his tower on the southern edge of Darkwood Forest.

NOW TURN OVER

1

For an old man, Yaztromo is surprisingly sprightly. You cross Red River and the ploughed fields beyond, and soon reach the edge of the forest. Yaztromo still doesn't stop. He takes a narrow path leading into the dark wall of trees. The light fades; branches and knotted roots obstruct the twisting path and make the walk very tiring. You ask Yaztromo why he seems unconcerned at the possibility of being attacked by forest monsters. He chuckles and tells you that his magic is well known and respected by all the creatures for miles around – none would dare challenge Yaztromo! After spending a peaceful night in the forest, you reach Yaztromo's tower by mid-morning the next day. You follow him up the spiral staircase to a large room at the top of the tower. Shelves, cupboards and cabinets line the walls and are filled with bottles, jars, books, boxes and all manner of strange artefacts. Yaztromo slumps down into his old oak chair, by now looking quite tired from the long journey. He reaches into his pocket and pulls out a fragile pair of gold-rimmed spectacles. After placing them on his nose, he peers at you over the top of them, and you feel quite unnerved by his piercing gaze. Finally he says, 'Anybody who would hope to defeat Malbordus must certainly know a little magic. You look bright enough to learn some, but I don't think you have time to absorb the ten spells I would like to teach you. By the way, I would like you to know how privileged you are to learn my magic. But a crisis is a crisis. Now, let's get on with it. Which spells shall I teach you? You have the choice of Open Door, Creature Sleep, Magic Arrow, Language, Read Symbols, Light, Fire, Jump, Detect Trap and Create Water.' To make your choice, turn to 34.

2

The room is small and sparsely furnished, with just a table and chair. A chisel and mallet are lying on the chair, and the floor is covered with wood-shavings. On the wall to your left is a large wooden carving, two metres by three metres in size. It depicts a scene of the lost city being attacked by Giant Sandworms. If you wish to take a closer look at the wood-carving, turn to 302. If you would rather walk through the door in the wall opposite, turn to 93.

3

The door opens into another corridor, which is well lit and appears to be in regular use. If you wish to go left, turn to 320. If you wish to go right, turn to 358.

4

The cool water quenches your thirst. You immediately feel invigorated, as the water contains rare strength-building chemicals. Add 4 STAMINA points. With water still running down your chin, you continue your search. Turn to 370.

5

You take one of the knives and place it in your backpack. Continuing down the corridor, you soon come to a dead end, and have no choice but to retrace your steps and walk under the golden rain. Turn to 354.

6

It is impossible to avoid stepping on some of the hundreds of cowrie shells. As you do so, all the shells suddenly cluster together and form themselves into an almost humanoid shape, which starts to attack you. You feel as though you are being stoned to death. Will you:

Try to defend yourself with your sword?	Turn to 245
Run away?	Turn to 359
Jump in the sea?	Turn to 51

7

On seeing you, the Lizard Man hisses loudly and advances towards you with his sword held high.

LIZARD MAN   SKILL 9   STAMINA 8

If you win, turn to 33.

8

You fall down, but land on the ledge overhanging the water. Lose 2 STAMINA points. You regain consciousness some time later and escape down the tunnel as quickly as possible. Turn to 91.

9

You raise the war-hammer into the air and bring it crashing down on top of the Dragon. It rebounds off it, leaving the artefact completely unmarked. You have chosen the wrong Dragon to destroy. You feel suddenly very weak as an unseen evil force tries to protect the artefact. Lose 1 SKILL point and 2 STAMINA points. Which Dragon will you now attempt to destroy?

The Bone Dragon?   Turn to 362
The Silver Dragon?   Turn to 231
The Gold Dragon?   Turn to 247
The Ebony Dragon?   Turn to 279

10

In the shimmering haze of the desert heat, you suddenly see a shape moving towards you. As it grows nearer, you see that it is somebody riding a camel. If you wish to speak to the desert rider, turn to 99. If you would rather lie low and wait until the rider has passed by, turn to 257.

11

If you are wearing a gold medallion with a heart engraved on it, turn to 258. If you are not wearing the medallion, *Test your Luck*. If you are Lucky, turn to 284. If you are Unlucky, turn to 71.

12

Yaztromo explains that his Open Door spell will open any locked door. He tells you the incantation necessary to cast the spell and says that it will not drain your energy too much; only 2 STAMINA points will be lost each time you use it. Return to 34, after writing down the spell and its STAMINA cost on your *Adventure Sheet*.

13

Another tentacle wraps itself around your other leg, and you gasp for air as you thrash around in the water trying to stab your unseen adversary.

TENTACLED THING   SKILL 8   STAMINA 10

You will drown if you do not slay the water monster in less Attack Rounds than the number of your current SKILL. If you win, turn to **165**.

14

Inside the pot you find a copper ring which has a lightning bolt engraved on it. Will you:

Place the ring on your finger?	Turn to 277
Lift the lid of the black pot?	Turn to 156
Lift the lid of the red pot?	Turn to 183
Walk through the chamber to the archway in the far wall?	Turn to 20

15

The night passes without incident; you wake at dawn feeling refreshed. Add 2 STAMINA points. You sling your backpack on to your shoulders and set off again (turn to 305).

16

The crossbow bolt thuds into your shoulder, making you cry out in pain. Lose 3 STAMINA points. If you are still alive, turn to 158.

17

The corridor ends at a doorway which is made of iron. You turn the handle and enter an empty room which has two doors leading from it – one to your left and one to your right. If you wish to open the door to your left, turn to 298. If you wish to open the door to your right, turn to 216.

18

You chip off one of the Sandworm's teeth, which may be useful as a weapon. You tuck it into your belt and continue south. You walk steadily on until the sun sinks below the western horizon. Under the cloudless sky, the desert quickly becomes very cold. If you are able to cast a Fire spell, turn to **177**. If you have not learnt this spell, turn to **395**.

19

You choose at random a tapestry with the pattern of a burning phoenix rising from the ashes. You quickly place it in your backpack and hurry down the corridor. Turn to **263**.

20

Beyond the archway, the corridor is well lit and in good order. There is no sand or dirt on the floor, and the statues and carvings on the walls show no signs of deterioration. The corridor soon ends at a door which, you discover, is open. You enter an empty room with one other door in the far wall and a trapdoor in the floor. If you wish to open the door, turn to **307**. If you wish to open the trapdoor, turn to **397**.

21

The door opens into a corridor at a T-junction. One passageway runs to the left and right of the door, and another begins immediately in front of you. You see nothing of interest either to your left or right, and you decide to walk directly ahead. Turn to **46**.

22

You point the mirror at the Night Horror, but it simply smashes it into fragments with another bolt from its rod. You have no choice but to attack with your sword. Turn to **85**.

23

You watch the crow fly back towards Yaztromo's tower before stepping on to the rope-bridge. The crew of the barge are not concerned by your sudden appearance and continue with their various tasks. After crossing the bridge, you continue south across the scrubland. After an hour or so, you see smoke rising in the east. If you wish to investigate the source of the smoke, turn to **316**. If you would rather continue south, turn to **159**.

24

You walk by the dry, white skeleton of some unknown large creature and notice the corner of a
wooden box jutting out of the sand inside the rib-
cage of the dead beast. If you wish to dig the box out
of the sand and open it up, turn to **283**. If you would
rather keep on walking, turn to **70**.

25

With much effort, you eventually haul yourself out
of the pit. You go over to the other archway and
walk under it. Turn to **315**.

26

As the day draws on, your thirst becomes almost
unbearable. If you possess a water canister, turn to
217. If you wish to and are able to cast a Create
Water spell, turn to **372**. If you have no means of
drinking, turn to **84**.

27

You hold the mirror in front of you, but the Wind
Elemental blows it out of your hand, and you watch
it shatter on the floor. Again you are thrown against
the wall. Lose 2 STAMINA points. Will you try:

A Phoenix Tapestry?	Turn to **229**
An Ebony Facemask?	Turn to **241**
Neither of these?	Turn to **312**

28

Thrusting your sword into the air, you try to cut down the giant insect, while it attempts to stab you with its long sting. Fight the Needle Flies one at a time.

	SKILL	STAMINA
First NEEDLE FLY	5	6
Second NEEDLE FLY	6	7
Third NEEDLE FLY	7	6

If you win, turn to **168**.

29

You lift the lid slowly, wondering what you might find inside. Much to your surprise and delight, you see a small ornament made of silver – a Dragon artefact! You put the Silver Dragon in your pocket and walk back down the tunnel to turn right into the new branch. Turn to **59**.

30

A glutinous creature known as the Iron-eater has dropped on to your head. Fortunately, it only eats metal and is harmless to human flesh. You scrape the thick jelly off your hair, but decide to leave the cellar anyway. You run back up the steps into the empty room and open the other door. Turn to **307**.

31

For over an hour you lie unconscious on the desert ground. *Test your Luck*. If you are Lucky, turn to **220**. If you are Unlucky, turn to **92**.

32

You utter the words of the spell (reducing your STAMINA by 1 point), but nothing happens. Unknown to you, the golden rain has drained away all your magic powers. Lose 1 LUCK point. You have no option but to use something from your backpack. Turn to **115**.

33

You tip open the sacks, but they contain merely spices and grain. A quick search through the Lizard Man's clothes produces a large iron key, which you slip into your shirt pocket. You move on and arrive at another T-junction. If you wish to go left, turn to **125**. If you wish to go right, turn to **262**.

34

Choose any of the following spells. You will be sent back to this reference after having learned a spell. As soon as you have learned four spells, turn to **180**. You think about the task ahead, before telling Yaztromo your choice.

Open Door	Turn to **12**
Creature Sleep	Turn to **58**
Magic Arrow	Turn to **136**
Language	Turn to **194**
Read Symbols	Turn to **391**
Light	Turn to **223**
Fire	Turn to **264**
Jump	Turn to **301**
Detect Trap	Turn to **342**
Create Water	Turn to **367**

35

You take each of the Dragons and place them on the floor. You look at them carefully and ponder their dormant power. Which Dragon will you attempt to crush first?

The Bone Dragon	Turn to 87
The Silver Dragon?	Turn to 126
The Crystal Dragon	Turn to 204
The Gold Dragon?	Turn to 62
The Ebony Dragon?	Turn to 324

36

Aboard your flying mount, you shout the words of the Magic Arrow spell (deduct 2 STAMINA points). A shimmering dart immediately appears on one of your fingertips and flies out to meet the diving Pterodactyl. The dart sinks deep into its underbelly, but does not kill it, and it swiftly closes in to attack (turn to 311).

37

You cast the spell (deduct 1 STAMINA point) and are suddenly able to read the symbols. A simple warning on the plaque reads DO NOT DRINK! But you decide that no harm can come to you if you just bathe your wounds. Turn to 269.

38

You carry on down the corridor, which finally leads into a large chamber lit by torches mounted on high walls. At the top the walls slope inwards to form a magnificent golden ceiling. A massive bronze idol stands in the middle of the chamber with its war-hammer raised. You will have to walk past the idol in order to reach the entrance of a tunnel in the far wall. If you walk to the left of the idol, turn to 291. If you walk to the right of the idol, turn to 381.

39

Long before noon, you are desperately thirsty. If you possess a water canister, turn to 63. If you can and wish to cast a Create Water spell, turn to 281. If you have no means of drinking, turn to 355.

40

The tapestries are large and colourful, depicting various gods and deities, some of whom are in human form, some in animal form, and a few are part human and part animal. If you wish to pull one of the tapestries from the wall and put it in your backpack, turn to 19. If you would rather walk past them, turn to 263.

41

There is nothing of interest among the Dark Disciples' possessions, apart from a long, sacrificial dagger which you place in your backpack. You see an archway in the wall behind the altar and decide to walk over to it. Turn to 341.

42

Stepping through the doorway over the body of the Serpent Guard, you find yourself in the middle of a deserted square. Turn to **111**.

43

As you make your way across the dusty floor to the door in the wall opposite, your mind suddenly fills with horrific images. You scream in terror, as you think you see the whole room become engulfed in flames. Your flesh appears to be burning and death seems imminent. Your nightmare drags on for five minutes before the strain makes you lose consciousness. You come to about an hour later, and when you try to stand up, you realize that you have lost some of your nerve and courage. Your hands still tremble and you feel completely shaken. Lose 3 SKILL points. You stagger towards the iron door in the far wall to leave the room of fear. Turn to **117**.

44

Through the semi-transparent drapes, you can just see a white-robed man enter the chamber, carrying a golden chalice. He is wearing a head-dress which is fastened by a gold clasp in the shape of a phoenix with its wings flat against his forehead. When the Priest sees the Slave Guard, he drops to his knees and presses his ear against the dead man's chest. Then he looks up and, after quickly surveying the chamber, runs out again without noticing you. Wasting no time, you set about opening the door. Turn to **336**.

45

Your burly opponent is a Pirate, well practised in swordsmanship. He quickly draws his cutlass from its scabbard as the eager crowd forms a circle around you.

PIRATE   SKILL 9   STAMINA 8

If you win, turn to **166**.

46

After walking for some fifty metres, your progress is halted by a deep pit which spans the width of the corridor. If you can and wish to cast a Jump spell, turn to **215**. If you are forced to jump the pit without magical aid, turn to **259**.

47

You run through the doorway into a cross passage. To your left you see Leesha at the end of the passage, opening an iron door. To your right, you see a Dwarf crawling towards you on his hands and knees. His face is red and blistered, and he appears delirious with sunstroke. He seems to recognize you, and calls out in a gruff voice. If you wish to keep chasing after Leesha, turn to 314. If you wish to speak to the Dwarf, turn to 171.

48

The body of the eagle shudders as it receives its death blow. You drop out of the sky like a stone and land fatally on the ground below. Your adventure is over.

49

The corridor ends at a T-junction. If you wish to go left, turn to 250. If you wish to go right, turn to 333.

50

You crack the clay pot open with the hilt of your sword and are surprised by the hissing sound of gas escaping. The box is a looted treasure chest, but the bandits did not fall for the trap that was left inside it. Your head is engulfed in a cloud of poisonous gas, which you cannot avoid inhaling. Lose 6 STAMINA points and 1 SKILL point. If you are still alive, turn to 31.

51

You run into the sea and dive below the surface, swimming underwater for as long as you are able to hold your breath. Only when your lungs feel as though they are bursting do you break the surface. You look back and see the Shell Monster hovering above the beach at the point where you jumped into the sea. You swim along the shoreline and scramble back on to the beach when the Shell Monster is out of sight. Two portions of your Provisions are sodden and no longer edible. You decide not to risk walking along the beach, so you head east inland (turn to **327**).

52

The acrid vapour becomes stronger, until you feel quite sick. The room begins to spin before your eyes and you cannot stop yourself from blacking out. Teetering on the edge of the pool, you fall over. *Test your Luck*. If you are Lucky, turn to **8**. If you are Unlucky, turn to **130**.

53

You do not waste any time searching the bodies of the Skeleton Men, but run through the archway into another chamber beyond. Turn to **119**.

54

You say the words of the spell (deduct 3 STAMINA points) and leap with ease over the wall. You land gently in the middle of a deserted square. Turn to 111.

55

The chair has many mysterious powers, and few dare sit on it. *Test your Luck*. If you are Lucky, turn to 286. If you are Unlucky, turn to 360.

56

The corridor turns sharply to the left again and soon you arrive at another T-junction. The corridor is bare and uninteresting straight ahead, so you decide to turn right. Turn to 46.

57

Another dollop lands just by your feet and the vapour rising from it smells sharp and acidic. Deciding that it would be dangerous to linger any longer in the dark cellar, you climb back up the steps and open the other door. Turn to 307.

58

Yaztromo explains that his Creature Sleep spell will put to sleep any humanoid creature. He tells you the incantation necessary to cast the spell and says that it hardly drains your energy at all, merely by 1 STAMINA point each time you use it. Return to 34, after writing down the spell and its STAMINA cost on your *Adventure Sheet*.

59

Ahead in the corridor you see a cloaked figure carrying a lantern and walking away from you. You call out, but the figure only walks away faster. You hurry after it and are almost alongside it when it spins around to reveal its hideous face. Taut yellow skin is stretched over its skull; its eyes are blood-red and sunk deep in their sockets. Surviving the stare of a Phantom requires great courage. Roll two dice. If the total is the same as or less than your SKILL, turn to **280**. If the total is greater than your SKILL, turn to **253**.

60

The bucket clatters to the stone floor when the rope is cut, spilling its contents – old bones – all around the room. Gathering them all together, you discover that one of them has been carved into the shape of a Dragon. This is one of the artefacts you have been seeking! You put the carved bone in your pocket and walk over to the door in the far wall. Turn to **21**.

61

You show the Gnome no mercy and run him through with your sword. You search through his room and find a purple silk purse inside a tin box. You open the purse and find a silver armband inset with a large emerald. If you wish to put on the armband, turn to 384. If you wish to climb back down the ladder and walk back past the last junction, turn to 262.

62

The artefact looks harmless lying on the floor, but you suspect that destroying it will not be an easy matter. If you are carrying a war-hammer, turn to 247. If you do not have this weapon, turn to 193.

63

You pour all the precious water into your mouth and gulp it down swiftly. Staring into the empty canister, you begin to regret your action. You have no choice but to carry on, but at least you feel refreshed (turn to 116).

64

In one of the boxes you find a gold medallion and chain which has a heart engraved on it. If you wish to put the medallion around your neck, turn to 163. If you would rather leave it in its box and walk back into the last room you entered to open the other door, turn to 298.

65

The reflection of its own gaze does not affect the Eye
Stinger, and it bears down on you. You drop the
Mirror on the floor and hear it shatter, as you hurry
to draw your sword. Lose 1 LUCK point and turn to
236.

66

You soon arrive outside another door. No noise
comes from the other side, but when you try the
handle, you find that the door is firmly locked. Will
you:

Cast an Open Door spell (if you are able to)?	Turn to **322**
Try to unlock it with a golden key (if you have one)?	Turn to **110**
Continue walking down the corridor?	Turn to **17**

67

The captain smiles as you hand him the gold, and
tells you that he hopes you will enjoy the river
journey. You shake hands and walk out of the cabin
(turn to **102**).

68

You chop furiously at the lock until it finally gives way. The door opens into a corridor, which you walk down until you reach two doors at the end. One door has the symbol of the sun in relief on it, and the other door bears the symbol of the moon. There are also strange signs carved below both the sun and the moon. Will you:

Cast a Read Symbols spell (if you are able to)	Turn to **255**
Open the Sun door?	Turn to **243**
Ø ZZ q	
Open the Moon door?	Turn to **273**
Ø↓⊔⌐→人田	

69

You reach into your backpack and give the handbell to the happy Gnome. He then opens a tin box, takes out a purple silk purse and throws it to you. You open the purse and pull out a silver armband which is inset with a large emerald. You place it on your sword-arm and say goodbye to the Gnome. Turn to **384**.

70

You have walked for only about an hour when the sun begins to set. The flat desert sand offers no shelter, and you are forced to sleep out in the open. The night passes without incident and you are soon on your way again. By mid-morning your thirst is great, and you long for a drink of water. You search around and suddenly see a bulbous green plant covered in sharp spikes, looking like a small, round cactus. If you wish to cut the plant open with your sword, turn to **120**. If you can and wish to cast a Create Water spell, turn to **345**. If you just wish to press on south, turn to **192**.

71

The Dark Disciples do not believe your story and close in to attack you with their sickles. Turn to **188**.

72

The desert quickly heats up and you are soon toiling under the white sun. Not far to the west, you see what looks like a cluster of trees with large birds circling above them. If you wish to walk over to the trees, turn to **142**. If you prefer to keep walking south, turn to **39**.

73

Leesha appears surprised that you have managed to enter her inner temple and defeat all her guards. She rises from her couch and steps towards you, holding aloft a shiny, black, crescent-shaped object. If you can and wish to fight her using a Giant Sandworm's tooth, turn to **219**. If you wish to attack her with your sword, turn to **282**.

74

You step into the tunnel and notice that the floor starts to slope downwards. It finally leads down to the edge of a flooded room. Water flows into the room through the mouth of a lion's head set in the wall. There is a ledge on the far wall which rises above the water, and the tunnel continues beyond it. You shrug your shoulders and wade into the murky water. You are waist-deep in the flooded room when a long tentacle breaks the surface. The water is stirred up as the monster thrashes around, sensing that food is near by. Suddenly another tentacle wraps itself around your leg and tries to drag you underwater. You draw your sword and begin hacking blindly at your attacker. If you are wearing a Bracelet of Mermaid Scales, turn to **396**. If you are not wearing this item, turn to **13**.

75

The vicious Harpy swoops down to attack you with its razor-sharp talons.

HARPY   SKILL 8   STAMINA 5

If you win, set off south again, keeping a watchful eye out for other hostile creatures (turn to **86**).

76

You crawl away from the pool, trying to escape the fumes, which make you feel sick. When you are at last able to stand, you head back down the corridor as fast as you can. Turn to **364**.

77

By the time you are clear of the broken glass, there is nobody in sight. The corridor stretches on, passing a stone archway on the left. Whoever threw the bottle did not run through the archway, so you continue straight on. The corridor finally ends at a T-junction, and you realize that you are unlikely to find your assailant now. Wondering if it was perhaps Malbordus taunting you, you ponder which way to turn. If you wish to go left, turn to **250**. If you wish to go right, turn to **333**.

78

Not far along the beach, you see a line of palm trees and make your way over to them. You find two coconuts on the beach and break them open with your sword. After gulping down the milk, you devour the soft white flesh inside the shell and lie down in the shade to rest. Add 3 STAMINA points. Checking through your belongings, you find that sea-water has seeped through the waxed paper wrappings of your Provisions. Roll 1 die and reduce your Provisions by the number rolled. If the number rolled is 3 or greater, lose 1 LUCK point as well. When you at last feel fit enough to walk, you stand up and decide which way to head. If you wish to walk east inland, turn to **327**. If you would rather walk south along the coast, turn to **151**.

79

The door opens into a candle-lit chamber which has a strong, musty smell. The floor is covered with debris – scraps of rotting food, matted hair, ash, teeth and animal droppings. When the door behind you closes, the door in front of you flies open, and a deformed, one-eyed mutant lumbers into the room, brandishing a silver rod. A bolt of white light shoots out from the rod and burns a black patch on the floor by your feet. The sun has set outside and the Night Horror is stalking the corridors of Vatos in search of prey. If you wish to use your sword against this loathsome creature, turn to **85**. If you would rather search through your backpack for some other weapon, turn to **309**.

80

The corridor soon turns right again and you reach an iron door in the right-hand wall. In the distance you can see glowing lights dancing about in the gloom of the corridor. If you wish to open the iron door, turn to **153**. If you wish to investigate the moving lights, turn to **339**.

81

The afternoon sun continues to beat down relentlessly, its intensity causing shimmering waves of heat to rise from the parched sand. Your mouth and throat feel as if they have been baked in a clay oven, and you begin to suffer the consequences of loss of water from your body. Lose 4 STAMINA points. Desperate to find water soon, you press on resolutely (turn to 24).

82

There is a scroll of paper inside the casket with a message written on it in dried blood, which reads, 'The Messenger of Death awaits you.' A shiver runs down your spine at the thought, and you tear the paper into shreds. Hurling the casket at the wall in a fit of rage, you look around and decide what to do next. Will you:

Help yourself to some of the gems?	Turn to 143
Take the golden skeleton statuette?	Turn to 386
Leave the room by the door opposite?	Turn to 3

83

The Gnome is grateful that you did not slay him. He tells you that he stumbled across Vatos many years ago and decided to stay. He is nothing but a scavenger these days, but he says he is quite happy. Vatos was deserted for many years, but gradually men and other creatures found it while seeking shelter, and a few of them stayed. There is no law in Vatos and nobody in control, although the most powerful usually get their way. Passing caravans are attacked for food, the raids being organized by a High Priestess and her slaves. You ask him if he has heard of Malbordus, but he shakes his head, saying, 'I don't take much interest in people. I just spend my time collecting and scavenging. Perhaps you have something to trade? I would give a lot for one of those fancy things that you look through to make other things seem a lot closer than they really are.' If you have a telescope to trade, turn to 138. If you do not have what the Gnome seeks, turn to 321.

84

The afternoon sun continues to beat relentlessly down, its intensity causing shimmering waves of heat to rise from the parched sand. Your mouth and throat feel as if they have been baked in a clay oven, and you begin to suffer the consequences of loss of water from your body. Lose 4 STAMINA points. Desperate to find water soon, you press on resolutely (turn to 303).

85

The Night Horror is a formidable opponent and is difficult to defeat with a sword.

NIGHT HORROR   SKILL 10   STAMINA 10

If you win an Attack Round, roll one die. If you roll between 1 and 3, your blow will not have harmed the Night Horror's undead flesh. If you roll between 4 and 6, your blow will wound it in the normal way. However, each Attack Round that the Night Horror wins, your STAMINA is reduced by 2 points, and your SKILL diminished by 1, because of the life-draining effect of the bolt. If your SKILL is reduced to 0, your life will be completely drained away and you will die. If you win, turn to **390**.

86

As you walk along, a leather pouch suddenly drops out of the sky on to the ground in front of you. You open the pouch and find a note inside, written by Yaztromo. It says: 'Friend, I have learned of bad news. Malbordus is already ahead of you. But look up, for help is at hand to enable you to catch up.'

Obeying his instruction, you look up and at first think another Harpy is above you, but then you see that it is a giant eagle, gliding through the air. The eagle circles above you and then lands with effortless ease close by. Pleased that old Yaztromo is concerned for your life, you climb on to the back of the eagle. You are soon riding through the air, travelling quickly towards the Desert of Skulls. However, your good fortune is quickly brought to an end when you hear an ominous screeching above you. Like a giant diving gannet, a hideous Pterodactyl swoops down to attack the eagle. If you are carrying a bow and arrow, turn to **132**. If you can and wish to cast a Magic Arrow spell, turn to **36**. If you do not possess a missile weapon, turn to **363**.

87

The artefact looks harmless lying on the floor, but you suspect that destroying it will not be an easy matter. If you are carrying a war-hammer, turn to **362**. If you do not have this weapon, turn to **193**.

88

The door opens into a room which is bare except for two stone caskets lying open on the floor. It is unnaturally cold in the room and the light is very dim. In the corner, you find a clay goblet with a heart etched inside the rim. You put the goblet inside your backpack and leave the room by the same door you entered, as there is no other exit. You walk back down the corridor and past the last junction. Turn to **250**.

89

You look around, but the old man is nowhere to be seen. Rummaging quickly through the robbers' pockets, you find a small brass telescope and three silver buttons. After packing away your finds, you set off again in search of a place to stay (turn to **379**).

90

You just manage to roll through the hole in the doorway as the stone ceiling meets the floor with a heavy thud. You pick yourself up and examine the room into which you have thrown yourself. Turn to 2.

91

Another tunnel branches off the one you are walking down, to give you a choice of directions. If you wish to continue straight on, turn to 347. If you would rather turn left along the new branch, turn to 59.

92

When you wake up, you feel terribly weak. Sitting up, you see footprints in the sand – and you did not make them. You hurriedly check your backpack and find that all your Gold has been stolen. Cursing your bad luck, you set off south again (turn to 70).

93

The door opens into a large hall which is lined with armour and weapons. At the far end of the hall there is an altar on a raised plinth, where three men with sallow skin are ceremoniously clothing themselves in dark brown robes. One of them sees you and signals to the others. They each pick up a sickle and advance towards you. They are Dark Disciples. If you wish to tell them that you have come with a gift for Leesha, the High Priestess of Vatos, turn to **11**. If you would rather fight them, turn to **188**.

94

After casting the spell (deduct 1 STAMINA point), you slowly begin to make sense of the pattern of the shells. It is a warning! The next two hundred metres of the beach is sacred ground, not to be walked upon by mortals. To do so would enrage the Demon of the beach. If you wish to ignore the warning and continue walking along the beach, turn to **6**. If you would rather journey east inland, turn to **327**.

95

The light quickly fades as you crawl along the tunnel, until you cannot see your hand in front of your face. Will you:

Cast a Light spell (if you are able to)?	Turn to **221**
Continue crawling in the dark?	Turn to **246**
Crawl back out of the tunnel, leave the room and walk up the corridor?	Turn to **344**

96

Just as you are about to walk through the archway into the chamber beyond, the Skeleton Men rise up from the floor. You can hardly believe your eyes, as they advance slowly towards you. Transfixed with fear, you cannot stop them thrusting their spears into your chest. You drop to your knees and fall face forward on to the floor. Your adventure ends here.

97

The helmet has been made by a skilful ironsmith. It will afford you greater protection. Add 1 SKILL point. Intent on finding the first Dragon artefact, you walk south along the corridor. Turn to **140**.

98

You enter a marble-floored room which is bare except for the bronze head of a beautiful woman mounted on the opposite wall. You are surprised when its lips suddenly start to move, and you hear her speak. 'Welcome to the room of question,' says the soothing voice. 'It has been an age since I last spoke to anyone. You are obliged to answer my question or die. Answer it correctly and you will be rewarded. Answer it incorrectly and you will suffer. Now tell me, how many Gold Pieces does Leesha give to the winner of the art competition?' If you know how many Gold Pieces make up the prize, turn to that number. If you do not know the answer, turn to 154.

99

On seeing you, the desert rider draws his sword and brings his camel to a halt. You call out, saying that you do not wish to fight him. You learn that he is on his way to join a merchant's caravan. You ask him if he has any water to spare and he offers to sell you a canister, but not for money. If you can and wish to trade either a silver button or a pearl for a canister of water, make the necessary adjustment on your *Adventure Sheet*. After bidding farewell to the desert rider, you set off east once again (turn to 257).

100

After only a few mouthfuls of the liquid, you feel horribly ill. Some of the herbs in the liquid are highly poisonous. Roll two dice and deduct the number from your STAMINA. If you are still alive, turn to **76**.

101

A feeling of terrible guilt overcomes you as you withdraw your sword from the dead man. You roll him over and see that he is clearly an outsider, perhaps sent here to help you. You try to convince yourself that he was either a treasure-hunter or an assassin, but the nagging doubts will not go away. Lose 2 LUCK points. But there is nothing you can do now except walk on. Turn to **80**.

102

The barge is neither very large, nor designed for paying passengers, but you find a coil of thick rope on which to lie. After your long walk, you are soon sound asleep, and do not wake until one of the crew taps you on the shoulder to say that Port Blacksand is in sight. You stand up and watch the sinister-looking city grow larger as you approach; ten minutes later you pass under a great arch to enter the city walls. The crew soon have the barge moored, obeying the frantic orders of the captain, who is obviously eager to load up his waiting cargo and leave before nightfall. You bid them all farewell and set about looking for a place to stay the night. The shadows start to lengthen as you walk through the narrow streets and alleyways. Suddenly, an old man in tattered clothes jumps out of a doorway and says, 'Looking for a bed, stranger? I know a good place that offers a room, soup and bread for only 1 Gold Piece. If you're interested, follow me.' If you wish to pay and follow the old man, turn to **332**. If you would rather keep looking on your own, turn to **379**.

103

Realizing that you are vulnerable to his magic powers, Malbordus draws his cursed sword and advances confidently. The sword has the ability to paralyse, and only your own swordsmanship can save you now.

MALBORDUS   SKILL 10   STAMINA 18

If you lose the first three Attack Rounds during combat, you will be paralysed by the evil sword, and Malbordus will triumph. Chaos will reign over Allansia. If you win the battle without losing three Attack Rounds, turn to **400**.

104

The arrow hits its large target, but does not kill the Pterodactyl. It squawks and turns away, but then dives down to attack again. If you wish to fire another arrow at the giant reptile, turn to **199**. If you would rather let the flying giants fight it out, turn to **311**.

105

The artist frowns and says, 'You've got awful taste. You wouldn't know the difference between art and an Orc's armpit!' If you wish to attack the impudent artist, turn to **123**. If you would rather leave him to his work and walk past him down the corridor, turn to **376**.

106

You suddenly see movement in the sand, being made by what looks like a large lizard. When it scurries closer, you see that its head is somewhat bird-like and its eyes are large and yellow like those of a toad. It is a deadly Basilisk. Will you:

Fight it with your sword?   Turn to **228**
Cast a Fire spell? (if you are
   able to)   Turn to **189**
Rummage through your backpack
   for another weapon?   Turn to **313**

107

The pouch contains nothing except a small golden key. You slip it into your pocket and continue your trek (turn to **10**).

108

On and on you walk under the searing desert sun. Late in the afternoon you see footprints in the sand leading from east to west across your path. If you wish to follow the footprints, turn to **205**. If you wish to keep walking south, turn to **303**.

109

Crawling blindly on, you do not see a tripwire, which you accidentally trigger with your arm. An unseen crossbow releases its bolt straight towards you. *Test your Luck.* If you are Lucky, turn to **16**. If you are Unlucky, turn to **368**.

110

The key fits the lock and it clicks open with one turn. Holding on to the hilt of your sword, you open the door. Turn to **98**.

111

Looking around, you see no sign of life. On the opposite side of the square there is a large stone archway. It seems as good a place as any to start your search for the Dragon artefacts. You walk through the arch to a stone stairway which descends to a torch-lit corridor below. As you walk warily down the stone steps, you wonder where Malbordus might be. At the bottom of the steps, you see an iron casket. If you wish to open the casket, turn to **287**. If you would rather walk south along the corridor, turn to **140**.

112

The grapes taste as good as they look, and they have also been grown for a special purpose. They contain magical healing properties. Add 4 STAMINA points. When you have eaten your fill, you walk on further down the corridor. Turn to **237**.

113

You draw your sword and run towards the murdering Dark Elves. Fight them one at a time.

	SKILL	STAMINA
First DARK ELF	5	6
Second DARK ELF	6	5

If you win, you find 2 Gold Pieces among the Elves' belongings, and you may take one of their bows and the two remaining arrows. After burying the poor man who was killed by the Elves, you set off south again (turn to **285**).

114

As you utter the words of the spell, the lock clicks open and you are able to push the door inwards. Reduce your STAMINA by 2 points for casting the spell, and turn to **88**.

115

The Elemental exhales loudly again, and once more you crash into the wall, as you try to rummage through your backpack. Lose 2 STAMINA points. Will you take from your backpack:

A Mirror?	Turn to **27**
A Phoenix Tapestry?	Turn to **229**
An Ebony Facemask?	Turn to **241**
None of these?	Turn to **312**

116

The sun's relentless heat beats down on you, but there is nowhere on the desolate landscape to offer you shade. If you are wearing a headscarf, turn to **289**. If you are bareheaded, turn to **275**.

117

The door opens into a corridor. Looking left, you see nothing of interest, but to your right, you see glowing lights dancing about in the gloom of the corridor. Curious to find out why the lights are moving, you walk towards them. Turn to **339**.

118

As you chant the spell, a shimmering dart appears on your fingertip and flies out to meet the diving Needle Fly. It is killed instantly. You quickly conjure two more darts and shoot the remaining two giant insects. (Remember to deduct 6 STAMINA points for casting the spell three times.) Turn to **168**.

119

You walk through the archway and up a flight of marble steps into a luxurious chamber, which has a high ceiling supported by parallel lines of marble pillars. Between the pillars there is a beautiful hand-woven red carpet which leads up to another short flight of steps. At the top of the steps, lying on a couch strewn with satin cushions, is a beautiful woman. She is being fanned by an ugly bald-headed creature. He has the muscular torso of a man, but his face is gaunt and his eyes are milky-white. You have entered the inner temple of Leesha. She smiles, snaps her fingers and her blind servant lumbers down the steps to attack you.

SERVANT   SKILL 8   STAMINA 8

If you win, turn to **73**.

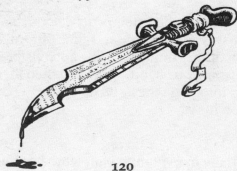

120

You cleave the top of the plant and see that it is filled with water. Carefully avoiding the spikes, you scoop out handfuls of cool water and soon feel refreshed. When you have drunk your fill, you set off south again (turn to **377**).

121

The bolt of light flies into your chest, knocking you back against the wall. Lose 2 STAMINA points and 1 SKILL point for its life-draining effect. What item will you pull from your backpack:

A Brass Handbell?   Turn to **198**
A Sandworm's tooth?   Turn to **331**
A Mirror?   Turn to **22**

122

You just fail to reach the far side of the pit, and bounce off its edge into the dark depths below. You land heavily some ten metres below, injuring yourself quite badly. Lose 6 STAMINA points and 1 SKILL point. If you are still alive, turn to **325**.

123

The artist makes no attempt to defend himself as you thrust your sword at him. But instead of wounding him, your sword hits an invisible shield. It jumps from your hand, turns and then flies with a dull thud into your chest. Its tip pierces your heart, killing you instantly.

124

Although the man bumped into you, he shouts and curses until the three flasks are filled again. Yet another Gold Piece is spent in paying for his drinks, and you begin to wonder how long your money will last. Lose 1 LUCK point. You finally manage to leave the bustling bar and lock yourself inside your room.

You wake at dawn after a restless night, scratching madly at inflamed bites from the bedbugs in your straw mattress. Wasting no more time in the Black Lobster, you make your way down the jetty to the *Belladonna* which, you notice, is flying the skull and crossbones – the flag of a pirate ship! Walking cautiously up the gangplank, you step aboard the ship (turn to **238**).

125

The corridor soon comes to a dead end, although there is a ladder leading up through a hole in the ceiling. If you wish to climb up the ladder, turn to **329**. If you would rather walk back down the corridor and continue straight on past the last junction, turn to **262**.

126

The artefact looks harmless lying on the floor, but you suspect that destroying it will not be an easy matter. If you are carrying a war-hammer, turn to **231**. If you do not have this weapon, turn to **193**.

127

You drop the burning medallion on to the sand and see a large letter M painfully branded on the palm of your hand. Fortunately it is not your sword-arm which is affected. Lose 1 STAMINA point. Realizing that Malbordus must be ahead of you, you continue south as quickly as possible (turn to **159**).

128

The door opens into a room which is empty apart from a large pile of bones lying in the corner. Scratch-marks on the wall appear to have been made by claws. You hear growling from a low arch in the far wall. Suddenly the door behind you opens and three large meat-covered bones are thrown into the room, before the door is slammed shut again. The growling becomes loud barking and suddenly a huge, slavering Death Dog bounds into the room. It sees you and immediately attacks.

DEATH DOG   SKILL 9   STAMINA 10

If you win, turn to 378.

129

When the sand-storm finally dies down, you see a shining object protruding from the sand. You reach down, tug on the object and discover that it is a brass handbell. You place it in your backpack and press on east (turn to 26).

130

You fall into the water with a resounding splash. You are not even conscious of your flesh turning soft and falling away from your bones. The water is now like concentrated acid because of its reaction with the blood of the Tentacled Thing. Your adventure is over.

131

You sit up with a start when you hear a deep humming coming from the corridor on the other side of the golden rain. There is a door behind the drapes, but it is locked and there is no time to open it. If you wish to hide behind the drapes, turn to **44**. If you wish to confront whoever is coming into the chamber, turn to **227**.

132

The diving Pterodactyl is a difficult target to hit, and you aim carefully before releasing the arrow. Roll two dice and add 3 to the total. If the total is the same or less than your SKILL, turn to **104**. If the total is greater than your SKILL, turn to **254**.

133

There is a sharp, acidic smell in the air as the jelly-like creature known as the Iron-eater begins to digest your helmet. You throw your helmet on to the floor and run back up the steps before your sword can be eaten. Fortunately, the Iron-eater does not harm human flesh. Lose 1 SKILL point for the loss of your helmet. Back in the empty room, you open the other door. Turn to **307**.

134

Aware of your dire predicament, you close your eyes and run at the Basilisk with your sword. But the Basilisk has another natural weapon – its venomous breath. Unable to see where to run, you are easy prey for the beast. You are soon lying dead, face down in the sand.

135

As you fumble to unlock the door, the crystal key falls from your fingers to the floor. It shatters on impact and you realize that all is lost. As the ceiling lowers relentlessly to the floor, there is a sickening crunch of bone. Your adventure ends here.

136

Yaztromo explains that his Magic Arrow spell will cause a small, shimmering dart to be fired from your fingertip with deadly accuracy at any target. He tells you the incantation necessary to cast the spell and says that it will not drain your energy too much; only 2 STAMINA points are lost each time you use it. Return to **34** after writing down the spell and its STAMINA cost on your *Adventure Sheet*.

137

The door leads into a hallway, at the end of which you see Leesha disappearing through another doorway. There is a bronze idol, in the shape of a dog, standing in the middle of the hallway. If you wish to stop and inspect the idol, turn to **186**. If you would rather follow Leesha, turn to **47**.

138

You take the brass telescope out of your backpack and dangle it in front of the Gnome to tease him. He starts to rub his hands together and snigger in excitement. He kicks a rug out of the way and starts to pull at a previously hidden iron ring that is attached to one of the flagstones. The stone lifts up to reveal a small chamber piled high with objects and items accumulated by the Gnome over the years. You rummage through and can hardly believe your eyes when you come across a small Crystal Dragon. It is one of the artefacts that you seek. You take it and give the Gnome the telescope. Bidding him farewell, you climb down the ladder and walk back down the corridor past the last junction. Turn to **262**.

139

If you are able to cast a Detect Trap spell, turn to **197**. If you do not know this spell, turn to **179**.

140

As you walk down the corridor, you suddenly feel a
light tap on your shoulder. You spin around and see
a horrifying creature with ragged clothes on its thin
body. Its hollow eyes and mouth are filled with
thick slime which makes its voice gurgle as it whis-
pers the word 'Death' in your ear. The Messenger of
Death then disappears, but somehow you know
what has happened. The Messenger of Death is a
sadistic killer who plays games with its victims.
Staying ahead of you, it will place each letter of the
word 'death' in various locations. Should you come
across and read all the letters of the word, the
Messenger of Death will reappear to revel in the
sight of your life draining away. Malbordus's assassin has given your search for artefacts an unwanted
twist. Turn to **330**.

141

You take a bunch of brass keys from the torturer's
belt and find the one to unlock the victim's mana-
cles. At first he is scared of you, believing it is a trick,
but gradually you convince him that you mean him
no harm. You learn that his name is Thitta, that he
was a servant of the High Priestess Leesha and was
caught trying to escape from Vatos. He asks you
why you are wandering about in the dungeon of
Vatos, and you tell him about Malbordus, the quest
and the Messenger of Death. His eyes widen and he
says, 'I saw a cloaked figure suddenly materialize
before my very eyes in the treasure-room where I
was hiding before being captured. I only saw its face

for a moment, and it was hideous. It put something inside a golden casket and then disappeared again.' Thitta declines the offer to accompany you on your mission, saying that he must try to escape again. You wish him luck and say goodbye. You leave the room together, but go your separate ways along the corridor. Turn to **66**.

142

As you get close, you see that the trees surround a pool of water. You have found an oasis. If you wish to drink the water, turn to **337**. If you wish to continue south without drinking, turn to **207**.

143

The gems are red-hot to the touch, although they do not emit any heat at a distance. *Test your Luck*. If you are Lucky, turn to **252**. If you are Unlucky, turn to **338**.

144

You seem to hang in the air for ages, but eventually land on the ground beyond the pit. You waste no time and continue straight on. Turn to **152**.

145

The bolt of light flies past your head and scorches the wall behind you. What item will you pull from your backpack?

A Brass Handbell?	Turn to **198**
A Sandworm's tooth?	Turn to **331**
A Mirror?	Turn to **22**

146

You tell the captain that you will offer him no more than 2 Gold Pieces. He scorns your offer, but after a few minutes of haggling, you agree on a fee of 3 Gold Pieces. You shake hands with the captain, pay him and walk out of the cabin (turn to **102**).

147

Unable to decipher the symbols, you decide to chase after whoever threw the bottle at you. Turn to **77**.

148

A thin figure in ragged clothing suddenly materializes in front of you. You begin to feel weak and sink to your knees; you sense that the Messenger of Death is revelling in your slow death. You have lost the chance to destroy the Dragon artefacts, and Malbordus will triumph. You have failed in your mission.

149

The struggle is over; both of your arms become entwined by the Sand Snapper's tentacles. Slowly you are dragged into the gaping mouth to be slowly digested. Your adventure comes to a horrific end.

150

The ceiling is descending fast, and you have to stoop while trying to fit the crystal key into the lock. *Test your Luck.* If you are Lucky, turn to **209**. If you are Unlucky, turn to **135**.

151

Not far down the beach, you notice a strange pattern in the sand, made from hundreds of cowrie shells. In the centre of the shells, skewered into the ground, is a spear adorned with sea-bird feathers. Will you:

Keep walking along the beach?   Turn to **6**
Turn east inland?   Turn to **327**
Cast a Read Symbols spell (if you
    are able to)?   Turn to **94**

152

In the gloom of the torch-lit corridor, you see a horrible creature hovering in the air and blocking your path. It is round, with a large eye in the centre of its dark green scaly skin, which is covered with spines. The Eye Stinger floats towards you, trying to mesmerize you with its hypnotic gaze and sting you with its spines. If you wish to fight the killer with your sword, turn to **236**. If you would rather look through your backpack for something to use, turn to **387**.

153

The door opens into a room lit by torches set in the wall. If you wish to walk across the dusty floor to an archway in the wall opposite, turn to **261**. If you would rather continue along the corridor towards the glowing lights, turn to **339**.

154

'I am disappointed in you, warrior,' continues the talking head, 'I had expected better.' Green smoke starts to pour from its mouth and you start to panic. Before you can reach the door, the smoke starts to swirl around your face, making you feel disorientated. Lose 3 SKILL points and 4 LUCK points. When the smoke finally drifts away, the bronze head is still and silent. You walk out of the room and up the corridor. Turn to **17**.

155

You crush the scorpion under your boot and carry on pulling away the rocks. In the middle of the rocks, you find a small white cotton sack, which is tied around a spherical object. If you wish to untie the sack, turn to **349**. If you wish to leave the tied sack among the rocks and continue south, turn to **39**.

156

Inside the pot you see a shrivelled paw, about the size of a monkey's. Will you:

Take the paw?	Turn to **318**
Lift the lid of the white pot?	Turn to **14**
Lift the lid of the red pot?	Turn to **183**
Walk through the chamber to the archway in the far wall?	Turn to **20**

157

The corridor soon ends at a T-junction. If you wish to go left, turn to **175**. If you would rather go right, turn to **353**.

158

You grit your teeth and pull the bolt out of your shoulder. You crawl painfully on down the tunnel, which finally opens out into a dusty room, lit by torches set in the wall. Turn to **43**.

159

The day wears on and you make good progress over the flat scrubland. When it is finally too dark to walk any further, you find shelter in a cluster of boulders. Roll one die. If you roll a 1, turn to **398**. If you roll any other number, turn to **15**.

160

There is a row of windows along the far wall, one of which is open. You hear a clap of thunder and walk over to the open window to look outside. The bright light hurts your eyes, and although the sun is shining it is suddenly blotted out by a dark shape in the sky. A huge, black Dragon soars overhead and you see an evil-looking man riding on its back. The Dragon roars and you can just hear the wicked laugh of Malbordus. The Dragon flies off north, and there is nothing you can do to stop it. Malbordus will lead his hordes of chaos across Allansia and the world will fall under a dark shadow. You have failed in your mission.

161

The mural stretches along the wall for approximately twenty metres and depicts a great battle. A mass of Undead, whipped on by vile Orcs, are pushing back an army of men and Dwarfs. The leader of the Undead is hidden by dark robes, apart from his fleshless, reptilian skull. His cold, evil, green eyes stare threateningly from the mural. He appears to be holding a casket which is drawing in the spirit of the king of the men and Dwarfs, for whom the battle seems lost. You are fascinated by the painted detail of the casket, and marvel at its magnificence. 'Do you like my work?' comes the sudden question from behind you. You spin round and see a man standing calmly with paint-pots in his hand and a brush behind his ear. He is smiling and seems pleased that you are showing interest in his work. Will you:

Attack him?	Turn to **123**
Reply to his question?	Turn to **296**
Push past him and walk on?	Turn to **376**

162

The bare corridor turns sharply left. After fifteen metres, you see a gauntlet lying on the stone floor. If you wish to put the gauntlet on your sword-hand, turn to **201**. If you would rather step over it and walk on, turn to **56**.

163

Nothing eventful happens when you place the medallion around your neck, but, unknown to you, the medallion was made to be worn around the necks of sacrificial victims. Lose 1 LUCK point. Finding nothing else of interest, you walk back into the last room you entered and open the outer door. Turn to **298**.

164

Staring into the shimmering haze, you see a high stone wall, less than half a kilometre away. Various stone towers and roofs inside the wall protrude above it. As you get closer, you see that wind-blown sand has drifted high against the wall and that no trail or track leads to the entrance gate, which is partly blocked with sand. 'Vatos!' a voice inside you shouts. If you wish to try to open the wooden side-door next to the entrance gate, turn to 382. If you can and wish to cast a Jump spell, turn to 54.

165

The water is now deep red with blood. Just as you are climbing out on to the ledge, the water turns suddenly black, and an acrid vapour rises from the surface. If you wish to stay by the edge of the water to see what happens next, turn to 52. If you would rather head on down the tunnel, turn to 91.

166

The crowd does not stop you untying the leather pouch which is hanging from the dead Pirate's neck. You leave the murmuring onlookers and climb the stairs to your room, where you lock yourself in. You open the pouch and find 2 Gold Pieces and a large pearl. You settle down to sleep and wake at dawn after a restless night. To your disgust, you find that you are covered with inflamed bites from the bedbugs in your straw mattress. Wasting no more time in the inhospitable Black Lobster, you make your way down the jetty to the *Belladonna* which, you see, is flying the skull and crossbones – the flag of a pirate ship! Walking cautiously up the gangplank, you step aboard the ship (turn to 238).

167

Your whole body shudders as a bolt of light zigzags out of the rod and shatters the lock on the door. But the weapon was not intended for mortals' use, and you suffer the consequences. Lose 1 SKILL point and 2 STAMINA points. You drop the rod on the floor and walk through the open door into another room. Turn to 2.

168

You step over the grounded Needle Flies and continue your trek. After half an hour's steady walking, you stumble upon a robed man lying face down in the sand. If you wish to stop to look inside a leather pouch clutched in the hand of the dead man, turn to 107. If you wish to keep on walking, turn to 10.

169

You slowly squeeze the other button and watch another bolt of light shoot out of the rod. But this time it hits the door and shatters the lock. Your body shudders a second time, and you realize that this weapon was not intended for mortals' use. Lose 1 SKILL point and 2 STAMINA points. You drop the rod on the floor and walk through the open door into another room. Turn to 2.

170

You boldly throw back the drapes, half expecting a sign of death to be revealed. But there is merely a plain iron door, which, when you turn the handle, turns out to be unlocked. Will you:

Open the door?	Turn to 365
Turn left along the corridor?	Turn to 335
Turn right along the corridor?	Turn to 162

171

You run to the Dwarf's side and learn that he is an envoy from Stonebridge, sent by Yaztromo. He has brought you the legendary war-hammer of Stonebridge, with which to smash the Dragon artefacts. Nothing other than a war-hammer can destroy the Dragons. He also tells you that a Mage told him that it is vital that the Dragon found nearest to the entrance to the catacombs must be destroyed first. The Dwarf's speech becomes more and more laboured until he finally slumps down on to the floor. There is nothing you can do to help the valiant Dwarf, but you feel more determined than ever to finish the mission successfully. Clutching the fabled war-hammer, you run down the passageway to the iron door through which Leesha disappeared. Turn to 314.

172

The Golem crashes to the floor, breaking into many pieces. Stepping over the pieces of stone, you make your way over to the tunnel entrance. Turn to 74.

173

The captain laughs and says, 'Wrong! Take the pirate away to be flogged and thrown over the side.' You are immediately seized, and must face your doom. Your adventure ends here.

174

You begin shouting at the top of your voice to drown out the mesmeric chanting, and draw your sword to attack the Dark Disciples. Turn to **188**.

175

You follow the corridor until it turns sharply to the right. On turning the corner, you see a tall reptilian creature wearing armour and holding a curved sword. The Lizard Man appears to be guarding some sacks that are piled up against the wall. If you can and wish to cast a Creature Sleep spell, turn to **232**. If you would rather fight the creature with your sword, turn to **7**.

176

Another dollop falls from the ceiling and lands on your head. If you are wearing a helmet, turn to **133**. If you are not wearing a helmet, turn to **30**.

177

You say the words of the Fire spell, and create a fire
large enough to keep you warm through the night.
Lose 1 STAMINA point for casting the spell. In the
early-morning light you continue your desert trek
(turn to 72).

178

Using your chosen method to unlock the door (if
you used the spell, deduct 2 STAMINA points), you
step through the doorway into another room. You
toss the silver rod back through the doorway and
hear the grating noise of the ceiling beginning to
lower again. Knowing that you are safe from attack
from behind, you look around the room you now
find yourself in. Turn to 2.

179

Unknown to you, the door is an illusion. There is a
pit in front of the wall where you believe the door to
be, and you fall to the bottom of it some ten metres
below. Roll 1 die and deduct the number rolled from
your STAMINA. If you are still alive, turn to 25.

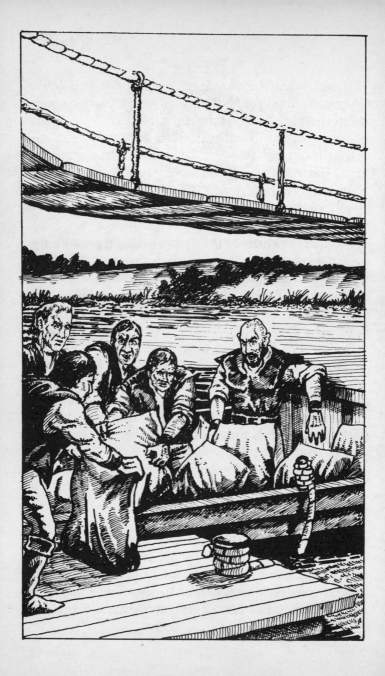

The old Wizard looks at you solemnly and says, 'Every minute is vital: you must begin your journey immediately. Without doubt, Malbordus will learn of your mission to thwart him and may send an assassin or two after you. My crow will lead you as far as Catfish River. From there you can either take a river vessel to Port Blacksand and then a sailing ship south, or journey overland to the Desert of Skulls. A grim task is ahead of you, but our thoughts will be with you.' Yaztromo leads you back down the spiral staircase and out into the open. Suddenly he gives a shrill whistle; a large crow immediately swoops down from the top of the tower and settles on his shoulder. 'Now, crow, guide our friend as far as Catfish River and make sure you keep a good look-out. The last thing we want is an ambush on our own doorstep.' You shake hands with Yaztromo and reassure him that you will destroy the Dragons of Vatos before Malbordus can attain his evil goal. He smiles and hands you a pouch containing 25 Gold Pieces. He then commands his crow to fly south. The crow squawks and flies off. You hurry after it, turning just once to wave goodbye to old Yaztromo. Walking through the tall grasses, a shiver runs down your spine at the thought of Malbordus's assassins coming after you. You travel steadily south, only deviating twice to circumvent danger spotted by the crow. Three hours later, you arrive at the banks of Catfish River at a point where it is spanned by a rope-bridge. An old barge is moored to a jetty beneath the bridge, and you see several rough-looking characters unloading sacks. If you wish to cross the bridge, turn to **23**. If you wish to buy your passage on the barge to Port Blacksand, turn to **213**.

181

The artist laughs and says, 'I never expected a compliment in this place of evil! No doubt you have been lured here with a promise of great wealth by the High Priestess, Leesha. I have staked my life on my reputation. Perhaps you have not heard that Leesha is a great lover of art, despite her cruel and terrible ways. Each year she secretly invites artists to perform their works inside the lost city. Down the corridor you will see tapestries, and elsewhere there are wood-carvings and etchings. She alone judges the works, and the result is final, very final. The winner receives 300 Gold Pieces, and the losers are sacrificed to honour the Dark One. Needless to say, I think I'm going to win. She gives us all a ring of protection to wear so that we come to no harm while we work. My name is Murkegg, and I'm pleased to meet you.' You ask him if he has heard of a man called Malbordus, but he shakes his head. You stress that it is very important that you find Malbordus, and ask if he has any knowledge of the tunnels and passageways. Murkegg rubs his chin and replies, 'I'm afraid I cannot help you much, as I spend most of my time painting. I do know that Leesha's inner temple can only be reached by walking through the curtain of golden rain. Perhaps whoever it is you are looking for is being entertained by Leesha. All I can do is wish you luck.' You shake hands with him and press on down the corridor. Turn to **376**.

182

Your thrusting sword sinks deep into the eye of your deadly adversary, sending it crashing to the floor. Sickening yellow fluid oozes out of its eyes and corrodes the stone floor, while emitting toxic vapours into the air. You hold your breath and run past the dying Eye Stinger. Turn to **340**.

183

The pot is empty, but fortune is not with you. The underside of the pot lid has the letter E written on it in charcoal by the Messenger of Death. Lose 4 STAMINA points and 1 LUCK point. You throw the lid on to the floor, but it is too late. Will you:

Lift the lid of the white pot?	Turn to **14**
Lift the lid of the black pot?	Turn to **156**
Walk through the chamber to the archway in the far wall?	Turn to **20**

184

You utter the words of Yaztromo's spell and a shimmering dart appears on one of your fingertips. The dart flies out and sinks deep into the chest of the flying Harpy. It is killed instantly, and drops to the ground with a thud. Reduce your STAMINA by 2 points for casting the spell. Keeping a watchful eye out for other hostile creatures, you continue your trek south (turn to **86**).

185

The Phantom snatches the pearl out of the air. Laughing at your pathetic attempt to slay it, the Phantom grabs your arm with its free hand and you are instantly paralysed. Lose 4 STAMINA points. By the time the feeling has returned to your limbs, the Phantom is well out of sight. Walking stiffly along the tunnel, you continue your search. Turn to **190**.

186

You notice that the idol's mouth is hinged, and you find that the lower jaw drops open when you pull down on its left ear. Inside the dog's mouth, you find an artefact that you have been seeking – a small Golden Dragon. You quickly place it in your pocket and chase after Leesha. Turn to **47**.

187

As the ship starts to sink, all the cannon crew run towards the wooden steps that lead to the upper deck. In the mad scramble to escape, you are clubbed on the back of the head. You fall unconscious to the deck and drown aboard the sinking ship.

188

The Dark Disciples let out a howl as they move forward to attack you. Fight them one at a time.

	SKILL	STAMINA
First DARK DISCIPLE	9	5
Second DARK DISCIPLE	8	6
Third DARK DISCIPLE	9	5

If you win, turn to 41.

189

Knowing that a single glance from the piercing eyes of the Basilisk is enough to kill you, you say the words of the Fire spell with your eyes closed. A defensive wall of fire suddenly flares up all around you and burns on until the Basilisk tires of waiting and moves on. Casting the spell costs you 2 STAMINA points. Only when you are certain that the Basilisk is far away do you let the flames die and walk on (turn to 108).

190

The tunnel finally ends at a T-junction. The cross passage shows signs of more frequent use. The walls are decorated with murals and tapestries and there are torches at regular intervals to give plenty of light. If you wish to turn left towards the murals, turn to **161**. If you wish to turn right towards the tapestries, turn to **40**.

191

When you reach the end of the corridor, you realize that it was not a shimmering curtain that you saw, but a fine spray of golden rain which cascades from a series of holes in the ceiling into a shallow trough in the floor. The corridor turns left at the point where the golden rain falls, and stretches to the left as far as you can see. If you wish to keep walking along the corridor, turn to **249**. If you would rather step through the golden rain, turn to **354**.

192

As you keep going, you have difficulty in walking in a straight line because of weakness caused by dehydration. Lose 4 STAMINA points. Only your determination to beat Malbordus keeps you going (turn to **377**).

193

You draw your sword and smash the hilt down on top of the Dragon. It rebounds off it, leaving the artefact completely unmarked. But you have made a fatal error in using your sword. Your joints start to stiffen and you feel your skin grow taut against your bones. Slowly your whole body petrifies until you are nothing more than a lifeless stone statue. Your adventure ends here.

194

Yaztromo explains that his Language spell will enable you to understand any creature you try to communicate with, no matter what tongue it speaks. He tells you the incantation necessary to cast the spell and says that the energy lost when using it is insignificant; merely 1 STAMINA point is lost each time it is cast. Return to **34** after writing down the spell and its STAMINA cost on your *Adventure Sheet*.

195

You concentrate on casting the spell, trying to blot out the chanting voices from your mind. The effort is great (deduct 1 STAMINA point), but you succeed, and the three robed figures fall to the ground, fast asleep. You waste no time and walk towards an archway in the wall behind the altar. Turn to **341**.

You are no more than ten metres from the tent, when suddenly the flap is thrown back by a fat bearded man in yellow robes, his fingers adorned with ornate gold rings. He does not attempt to threaten you, but beckons you inside his tent, saying, 'Stranger, you look in need of a rest. Please accept my hospitality. I may even tempt you to buy some of my exotic wares.' Sensing no apparent danger, you step inside his tent and squat down on top of a rug. The nomad, whose name, you learn, is Abjul, gives you food and water which makes you feel much stronger. Add 4 STAMINA points. Abjul then smiles and says, 'Now, what will you buy, my friend?' He goes into great raptures about all the goods he has to sell, which you finally learn are as follows:

Sealing-wax	2 Gold Pieces
Onyx Egg	3 Gold Pieces
Ivory Beetle Charm	2 Gold Pieces
Bracelet of Mermaid Scales	3 Gold Pieces
Silver Mirror	4 Gold Pieces
Crystal Key	3 Gold Pieces
Ebony Facemask	3 Gold Pieces
Bone Flute	2 Gold Pieces

If you can and wish to buy any of Abjul's goods, make the necessary adjustment on your *Adventure Sheet*. Abjul tells you that he thinks Vatos lies in the southern part of the Desert of Skulls, and you decide to take his advice. Thanking him for his help, you set off south (turn to 389).

197

An inner voice tells you to say the words of the spell (deduct 2 STAMINA points). Suddenly you see that the arch does not exist at all. It is merely an illusion, hiding a pit in front of the wall. You detect that the other arch is genuine, and you walk through it. Turn to **315**.

198

You ring the bell and watch with pleasure as the Night Horror drops its rod and tries to cover its ears with its deformed hands. It screams in silent agony, and then collapses on to the floor. But your delight is short-lived, because you hear a grating sound above you. The silver rod, out of the hands of its owner, has magically triggered a mechanism in the stone ceiling which is starting to lower on top of you. You run to open one of the doors, but both are firmly locked and cannot be opened, even by Yaztromo's spell. Will you:

Pick up the silver rod?	Turn to **290**
Try a crystal key in the door (if you have one)?	Turn to **150**
Try to burn a hole in the door with a Fire spell (if you know it)?	Turn to **239**

199

As you reach into your backpack for another arrow, the eagle climbs steeply into the sky to out-manoeuvre the Pterodactyl. You grab its feathers to stop yourself from falling off its back and, in so doing, drop your bow. You watch it spiral down to the ground, and now you can do no more than await the outcome of the battle about to commence (turn to 311).

200

Finding nothing that you think might destroy the Eye Stinger, you decide to rely on cold steel and draw your sword. Turn to 236.

201

Unknown to you, the gauntlet is cursed and will lessen your dexterity. Lose 1 SKILL point. Unaware of your disability, you walk on. Turn to 56.

202

As you walk along, you suddenly notice the pungent smell of herbs in the air. It grows stronger as you approach the end of the corridor, where there is a crescent-shaped pool. There is a brass plaque attached to the wall with strange symbols etched on it which read Ø乙 人乙Γ Ø← →人+ Will you:

Cast a Read Symbols spell (if you are able to)?	Turn to 37
Drink some of the herbal liquid?	Turn to 100
Bathe your wounds in the herbal liquid?	Turn to 269
Walk back down the corridor?	Turn to 364

203

'I'll show you who's clumsy!' snarls the short-tempered man as he smashes the flasks into your face. Lose 1 STAMINA point. If you wish to fight the man, turn to 45. If you would rather save your anger for Malbordus and make your way to your room, turn to 251.

204

The artefact looks harmless lying on the floor, but you suspect that destroying it will not be an easy matter. If you are carrying a war-hammer, turn to **9**. If you do not have this weapon, turn to **193**.

205

Before long, you reach the body of a man lying face down in the sand. There is no blood, or any other sign of him having been attacked, and yet he is dead, despite having a water canister which is only half empty. There is a look of agony on the dead man's face, as if he had witnessed something inexplicably terrible. There is nothing belonging to the man which is of any use to you, apart from the water canister. You place it in your backpack and head south again (turn to **303**).

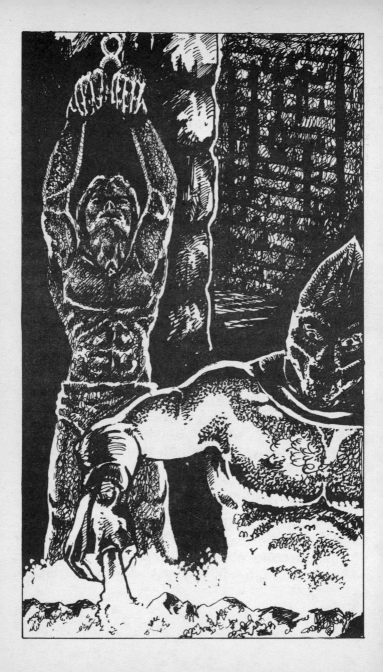

206

The door opens into a room which is filled with all kinds of implements of torture. The screaming is coming from a man who is hanging from the ceiling by his wrists, and the laughter is coming from his torturer, a hooded, bare-chested man who is holding a smoking branding iron. If you wish to help the unfortunate captive, turn to **328**. If you would rather leave him at the mercy of the torturer, and continue up the corridor, turn to **66**.

207

You suddenly stumble upon a large pile of rocks partly hidden by the wind-blown sand. If you wish to inspect the rocks, turn to **375**. If you would rather walk past them, turn to **39**.

208

As you utter the words of the spell (deduct 1 STAMINA point), the symbols begin to make sense. Too late you realize that it is a curse of bad luck, taken from a Mummy's tomb. Lose 4 LUCK points. Enraged, you chase after whoever threw the bottle at you. Turn to **77**.

209

The key turns in the lock and you are able to open the door just as the ceiling reaches the height of the handle. You crawl through the small space and examine the room you find yourself in. Turn to **2**.

210

There is no alternative but to try to force the door open with your sword. As you begin to hack at the lock, you become aware of a hissing sound coming from the other side of the door. Suddenly the door is pulled open and you are confronted by a strange, snake-like creature with a humanoid upper torso, which is protected by armour. A Serpent Guard is a vicious killer, and you are forced to draw your sword in an attempt to survive.

SERPENT GUARD   SKILL 10   STAMINA 10

If you win, turn to 42.

211

Skeleton Men are fanatics, who always fight to the death. They will be difficult to defeat.

	SKILL	STAMINA
First SKELETON MAN	9	6
Second SKELETON MAN	9	8

Fight them one at a time. If you win, turn to 53.

212

You find a small silver box inside the alcove which has a Dragon motif etched into the lid. Something inside rattles when you shake the box. If you wish to open the box, turn to 29. If you would rather replace the box in the alcove, walk back down the tunnel and turn right into the other branch, turn to 59.

213

After watching the crow fly back towards Yaztro-mo's tower, you follow the path to the jetty and walk confidently up to the first crewman you come to. You ask to talk to the captain. He eyes you suspiciously and after a long pause says, 'Follow me.' He leads you on to the barge and knocks hesitantly on one of the cabin doors. A gruff voice shouts, 'Enter!' The crewman opens the door and gestures at you to enter the cabin. You stride into the cabin and see a stocky man dressed in clothes that have seen better times. He asks you your business and you tell him that you wish to buy your passage to Port Blacksand. 'Anybody who would pay to get to the city of thieves must be either desperate or insane,' he says, laughing. 'It will cost you 5 Gold Pieces!' If you wish to pay the captain his asking price, turn to **67**. If you wish to haggle, turn to **146**.

214

After placing the coin in the slot, a panel in the door flaps up, revealing, much to your horror, the letter T scratched on its reverse side. The Messenger of Death has struck a blow. Lose 4 STAMINA points for the shock to your system. You curse the evil game and walk through the doorway. Turn to **268**.

215

You utter the words of the spell (deduct 3 STAMINA points) and leap over the pit with ease. Landing gently on the far side, you set off along the corridor. Turn to **152**.

216

The door opens into a storeroom which is filled with vases, urns, rugs, boxes, cushions and chests. As you walk in, the door slams shut behind you and a sinewy, horned beast with red skin suddenly climbs out of one of the urns and starts to spit fire at you. The Fiend is guardian of the storeroom and you must fight it.

FIEND   SKILL 6   STAMINA 8

In addition to its attack with claws and teeth, roll one die every Attack Round for its fiery breath. On a roll of 1 or 2, it burns you and causes an additional 1 point of damage to be subtracted from your STAMINA. On a roll of 3–6, you avoid the blast. If you win, turn to 233.

217

You take a long gulp of delicious water, savouring the brief moment when your mouth does not feel as dry as the desert sand all around you. The afternoon sun continues to beat down relentlessly, its intensity causing shimmering waves of heat to rise from the parched sand. You resist the temptation to finish off the water, and you press on (turn to 303).

218

In the pocket of one of the Rat Men, you find 3 Gold Pieces and a monkey's tail. In the far wall you see two arches and corridors running from them. If you walk through the left arch, turn to 315. If you walk through the right arch, turn to 139.

219

Leesha's facial expression changes suddenly from one of smug superiority to a look of horror. Invulnerable to ordinary weapons, her only weakness is being attacked with the jagged edge of a Giant Sandworm's tooth. On seeing your weapon, she flees from the temple through a door in the wall behind the couch. If you wish to open the chest lying beside the couch, turn to **265**. If you would rather run through the doorway after Leesha, turn to **137**.

220

When you wake up, you feel terribly weak. But the thought that Malbordus may now be ahead of you brings you to your feet. With grim determination, you stagger on south (turn to **70**).

221

You utter the words of the spell (deduct 2 STAMINA points), and the tunnel is immediately lit by magical light. You crawl on and see a crossbow attached to the wall further down the tunnel, with a tripwire two metres in front of it. You climb over the wire without triggering it, and squeeze past the mounted crossbow. The tunnel finally opens out into a dusty room lit by torches set in the wall. Turn to **43**.

222

The claws dig deep into your flesh and draw blood. The monkey's paw is cursed and will drain the spirit of all those except the Undead. Lose 2 SKILL points. You wrench the paw from your hand and drop it back in the pot. Will you:

Lift the lid of the white pot?	Turn to **14**
Lift the lid of the red pot?	Turn to **183**
Walk through the chamber to the archway in the far wall?	Turn to **20**

223

Yaztromo explains that his Light spell will illuminate any room, cavern or area, whether its darkness is natural or magical. He tells you the incantation necessary to cast the spell and says that the energy drained when casting it is not too much; only 2 STAMINA points are lost each time you use it. Return to **34** after writing down the spell and its STAMINA cost on your *Adventure Sheet*.

224

You utter the words of the Light spell (reducing your STAMINA by 2 points), but the spell does not work and the gloom is unbroken. Unknown to you, the golden rain drained all your magical powers. If you wish to descend further into the gloom, turn to **348**. If you would rather climb back up the steps and open the other door, turn to **307**.

225

You lunge at the Phantom, but your sword meets no resistance. Unaffected by normal weapons, the Phantom laughs at your pathetic attempts to slay it. It grabs your arm and you are instantly paralysed. Lose 4 STAMINA points. By the time the feeling has returned to your limbs, the Phantom is well out of sight. Walking stiffly along the tunnel, you continue your search. Turn to **190**.

226

You step on to the black patch and pick up the bronze medallion. Although it feels cold to the touch, you see with horror that the flesh on your hand is burning. *Test your Luck.* If you are Lucky, turn to **127**. If you are Unlucky, turn to **323**.

227

You stand against the wall, gripping your sword. A man in white robes enters the chamber carrying a golden chalice. He is wearing a white head-dress which is fastened by a golden clasp in the shape of a phoenix with its wings flat against his forehead. When the Priest sees the Slave Guard, he drops to his knees and presses his ear against the dead man's chest. Suddenly he looks up and sees you, and calls out in a loud voice, 'Barrabang Hinpo Garrabang.' Smoke rises from the golden chalice and forms into the shape of a fat humanoid. The Priest has summoned a Wind Elemental to kill you. The Elemental's cheeks puff up and the force of its exhalation sends you flying against the wall. Lose 2 STAMINA points. Your sword will not harm the Elemental and you must use something else to combat it before you are battered to death. If you can and wish to use a Fire spell, turn to **32**. If you wish to use something from your backpack, turn to **115**.

228

You do not even raise your sword against the Basilisk, for a single glance from its piercing eyes is enough to kill you.

229

The Priest instantly recognizes the tapestry and the significance of the Phoenix. He calls out a few words and the Wind Elemental recoils into the golden chalice. Realizing that you have the advantage, you tell the Priest that the Slave Guard was killed because he was planning to assassinate Leesha. Acknowledging your superiority, the Priest apologizes for his unwarranted attack, bows and walks back under the golden rain to leave the chamber. You waste no time and pull back the drapes to open the door. Turn to **336**.

230

You swim furiously towards the man-of-war and wave your arms to attract attention. A rope is thrown down to you and you haul yourself on to the victor's ship. Much to your surprise, the crew are made up entirely of Dwarfs. The captain questions you and other members of the sunken *Belladonna*'s crew, who have also been brought aboard. You tell the captain that you are on an important mission which started at the Dwarf village of Stonebridge.

The captain eyes you suspiciously, accusing you of being no more than a desperate pirate. 'So you say you started your quest in Stonebridge,' says the captain. 'If that is the case, tell me who is their king.' If you reply that his name is Gallibrin, turn to **173**. If you reply that his name is Gillibran, turn to **278**.

231

You raise the war-hammer into the air and bring it crashing down on top of the Dragon. It rebounds off it, leaving the artefact completely unmarked. You have chosen the wrong Dragon to destroy. You feel suddenly very weak as an unseen evil force tries to protect the artefact. Lose 1 SKILL point and 2 STAMINA points. Which Dragon will you now attempt to destroy?

The Bone Dragon?   Turn to **362**
The Crystal Dragon?   Turn to **9**
The Gold Dragon?   Turn to **247**
The Ebony Dragon?   Turn to **279**

232

Uttering the words of the spell, you watch with amusement as the angry Lizard Man suddenly drops sound asleep on the floor. Reduce your STAMINA by 1 point for casting the spell, and then turn to **33**.

233

There is no other way out of the room except by the way you entered. If you wish to search through the storeroom, turn to **64**. If you would rather leave straight away and open the other door in the last room you entered, turn to **298**.

234

You tap the glass ball on one of the rocks and watch it break open like an egg. The tiny Sprite flies out, rejoicing at the top of his almost inaudible high-pitched voice. He thanks you over and over again for releasing him from the entrapment spell. He sprinkles some sparkling dust on your head and says it will bring you good fortune. Add 1 LUCK point. He also advises you to make a headscarf out of the sack and cord to keep the sun off your head, as it is still a long way to Vatos. As you begin to tear open the sack, the Sprite waves and flies away. With your head and neck protected, you stride off south (turn to 39).

235

It is now far into the night, and the strenuous efforts of the day have left you feeling tired and thirsty. You find a bowl of water on one of the tables, which you empty down your throat in seconds. Too fatigued to go on, you lie down in the corner of the room on the soft, inviting cushions, in order to rest. If you let yourself fall asleep, turn to 267. If you stay awake, turn to 131.

236

Trying desperately to avoid the Eye Stinger's gaze, you cut blindly through the air with your sword. *Test your Luck*. If you are Lucky, turn to 182. If you are Unlucky, turn to 299.

237

The corridor ends at an archway which is covered by a black curtain. There is a skull carved out of the stone above the archway. Despite its ominous appearance, you throw back the curtain and step through the archway. You enter a small chamber which appears to be the annexe of a larger chamber beyond the archway in the wall opposite. But your immediate concern is with the creatures who are standing guard on either side of the archway. They have human bodies and skeletal heads. Each wears a strange helmet in the shape of a Sphinx. In a rasping voice, one of the Skeleton Men confronts you, saying, 'Give good reason to intrude on the domain of Leesha, or die.' Both of them stride towards you with their spears pointed at you. Will you:

Cast a Creature Sleep spell (if you are able to)?	Turn to 371
Tell them that you have brought Leesha a Giant Sandworm's tooth (if you have one)?	Turn to 294
Attack them with your sword?	Turn to 211

238

You walk around the ship until you find Gargo. He tells you that one of his gunners was killed in a tavern brawl last night, and that you will have to take his place. Your job will be to load cannonballs during battle. You are taken below deck and shown your hammock. Soon the *Belladonna* sets sail and you are pleased that at last you are heading south. In mid-afternoon there is a sudden shout from the crow's-nest, 'Ship on the starboard bow!' The ship is suddenly bustling with the crew running about their duties. The captain shouts his orders and everybody runs to their battle-stations. Wondering who the enemy might be, you take your place at your cannon. You hear the bad news that the enemy is a man-of-war and not a merchant ship. Noise suddenly erupts all around as the man-of-war's cannonballs smash into the *Belladonna*. The order is given to fire, but you realize that the *Belladonna* is no match for the battleship. In the course of the fierce battle, the *Belladonna* starts to sink and you fear for your life. Roll two dice. If the total is the same or greater than your SKILL, turn to **187**. If the total is less than your SKILL, turn to **308**.

239

The ceiling is lowering fast and you are on your hands and knees by the time the spell is cast (deduct 2 STAMINA points). The door suddenly bursts into flames and you hurl yourself through the hole that is made. *Test your Luck.* If you are Lucky, turn to **90**. If you are Unlucky, turn to **356**.

240

When the Gnome sees your drawn sword, he taps his pole on the floor three times in quick succession. It transforms before your eyes into a hissing serpent which slithers along the floor towards you.

SERPENT   SKILL 6   STAMINA 6

If you lose any Attack Rounds, turn to **373**. If you win without losing any Attack Rounds, turn to **270**.

241

You quickly pull the mask over your face, hoping to repel the Wind Elemental. But it has no effect at all, and you are blown back against the wall. Lose 2 STAMINA points. Will you try:

A Mirror?	Turn to 27
A Phoenix Tapestry?	Turn to 229
Neither of these?	Turn to 312

242

Seizing the Pterodactyl in its sharp talons, the eagle tears at its neck with its sharp curved beak. The Pterodactyl's death squawk grows fainter, as the huge flying reptile plummets to the ground like a stone. You cheer the valiant eagle as it continues to fly south. After flying over Whitewater River, the terrain becomes gradually more arid. When you at last reach the edge of the desert, the eagle flies down to land. It is dusk and the eagle does not intend to fly into the desert. You dismount and look around for a place to shelter, and opt for a hollow in the crusty sand. You awake soon after dawn, but are disheartened to find that the eagle has flown off home. You stare out into the desert landscape and see nothing but barren sand. Wondering what fate will befall you in the wilderness, you start the long walk south. As the sun rises, it quickly becomes uncomfortably hot. By noon, your mouth is parched and your thirst is unbearable. If you are able to cast a Create Water spell, turn to **297**. If you have not learned this spell, turn to **81**.

243

The door opens into a narrow corridor which grows hotter as you proceed along it. You start to sweat profusely and realize that you can go no further. You turn to go back, but flames have started to shoot from the cracks between the stones in the walls and floor. You are trapped in the corridor of fire. The sign under the sun symbol read DOOM, and the warning came true. Your adventure ends here.

244

Hoping to find something that might be effective against the Phantom, you thrust your hand into your backpack. What will you throw at the Phantom:

A Pearl?	Turn to **185**
A Silver Button?	Turn to **350**
An Ivory Beetle Charm?	Turn to **317**
None of these?	Turn to **260**

245

Your sword cuts through the Shell Monster easily, but does not appear to harm it. It continues to lash you and you reel back under its constant barrage. Lose 4 STAMINA points. You realize that you cannot harm it. If you wish to run away, turn to **359**. If you wish to run into the sea, turn to **51**.

246

If you are able to cast a Detect Trap spell, turn to **388**. If you do not know this spell, turn to **109**.

247

You raise the war-hammer into the air and bring it crashing down on top of the Dragon. It rebounds off it, leaving the artefact completely unmarked. You have chosen the wrong Dragon to destroy. You suddenly feel very weak as an unseen evil force tries to protect the artefact. Lose 1 SKILL point and 2 STAMINA points. Which Dragon will you now attempt to destroy?

The Bone Dragon?	Turn to 362
The Silver Dragon?	Turn to 231
The Crystal Dragon?	Turn to 9
The Ebony Dragon?	Turn to 279

248

As you whisper the words of the Open Door spell, with your parched mouth, the door swings slowly inwards. Deduct 2 STAMINA points for casting the spell. You step through and find yourself in the middle of a deserted square. Turn to 111.

249

Walking along the corridor, you suddenly see movement in the shadows. A muscular figure wearing leather armour is striding towards you. The torch light bounces off two long knives which the figure is brandishing. As the light falls on its head, you see that its skin is green and pock-marked, and that it has red eyes, flared nostrils and a wide mouth with needle-like teeth. In a deep guttural voice it says, 'Malbordus will triumph, and you will die.' The Mutant Orc Assassin has been sent to slay you.

MUTANT ORC   SKILL 11   STAMINA 11

Unless you are armed with a dagger in addition to your sword, you will be at a disadvantage against the trained killer with its two long knives. Reduce your Attack Strength by 2 points during each Attack Round. If you win, turn to 5.

250

You pass a doorway in the left-hand wall which has an ornately carved surrounding of hideous creatures being consumed by flames. If you wish to open the door, turn to **128**. If you would rather keep on walking, turn to **344**.

251

To the jeers of the crowd, you make your way towards the stairs. Following the example of the burly man, the crowd pushes and jostles you until you reach your room. Once inside, you lock the door, but find to your horror that you have had your pockets picked during the commotion. All your remaining Gold Pieces have been stolen. Lose 2 LUCK points. You settle down to sleep, cursing your luck, and wake at dawn after a restless night. To make matters worse, you find that you are covered from head to toe with inflamed bites from bedbugs in your straw mattress, and you start to scratch madly. Wasting no more time in the inhospitable Black Lobster, you make your way down the jetty to the *Belladonna*, which you see is flying the skull and crossbones – the flag of a pirate ship! Walking cautiously up the gangplank, you step aboard the ship (turn to **238**).

252

Fortunately it is not your sword-hand which is burnt. Lose 1 STAMINA point. You withdraw your hand quickly and decide what to do next. Will you:

Take the golden skeleton statuette?	Turn to **386**
Open the golden casket?	Turn to **82**
Leave the room by the door opposite?	Turn to **3**

253

With its powerful stare, the Phantom paralyses you before making its escape down the tunnel. Lose 4 STAMINA points. By the time feeling has returned to your limbs, the Phantom is well out of sight. Walking stiffly along the tunnel, you continue your search. Turn to **190**.

254

The arrow misses its target and the Pterodactyl closes in to attack (turn to **363**).

255

You utter the words of the spell (losing the STAMINA point), but nothing happens. Unknown to you, the golden rain has drained away all your magical powers. Now you must decide which door to open. If you wish to open the Sun door, turn to **243**. If you wish to open the Moon door, turn to **273**.

256

The parchment is inscribed with strange symbols which you do not understand. If you are able to cast a Read Symbols spell, turn to **208**. If you cannot cast this spell, turn to **147**.

257

Quite unexpectedly, the wind starts to blow and the sky grows dark. The wind becomes a howling gale and whisks up the sand, making it almost impossible to see. You are stranded in the middle of a sand-storm. Lose 2 STAMINA points and *Test your Luck*. If you are Lucky, turn to **129**. If you are Unlucky, turn to **385**.

258

The Dark Disciple nearest to you spots your medallion and says, 'Step forward. It is an honour for you to be sacrificed. The gift of your life will certainly please Leesha.' The three of them raise their arms and start to chant, and you feel compelled to walk up to the altar and lie down on the marble slab. If you can and wish to cast a Creature Sleep spell, turn to **195**. Otherwise, turn to **392**.

259

You stand back and take a running jump over the pit. Roll two dice. If the total is the same as or less than your SKILL, turn to **144**. If the total is greater than your SKILL, turn to **122**.

260

Finding nothing that you think might destroy the Phantom, you reach for your trusty sword. Turn to **225**.

261

As you step through the dust, your mind suddenly fills with horrific images. You scream in terror, as you think you see the whole room become engulfed in flames. Your flesh appears to be burning and death seems imminent. Your nightmare drags on for several minutes, and you fall unconscious under the strain. When you finally come to, you still feel terrified and your hands are trembling. Some of your courage is lost for ever. Lose 3 SKILL points. Not daring to venture any further in the room, you exit by the iron door. Back in the corridor, you stagger towards the dancing lights. Turn to **339**.

262

The corridor eventually opens into a dingy room in which two Rat Men are busily chewing on the carcass of a Goblin. On seeing you, they spring to their feet and attack you with their swords.

	SKILL	STAMINA
First RAT MAN	5	4
Second RAT MAN	5	5

If you win, turn to **218**.

263

The corridor runs straight, and you follow it until you reach a magnificent chair set against the left-hand wall, carved in the shape of a Sphinx. If you wish to rest in the chair, turn to **55**. If you would rather press on, turn to **202**.

264

Yaztromo explains that his Fire spell can be used to either make a defensive wall around the caster, or simply to ignite a torch or lantern with your finger-tips. He tells you the incantation necessary to cast the spell, and says that the energy lost when casting the spell will vary according to the intensity of fire required, but will use either 1 or 2 STAMINA points each time. After noting down the spell and its STAMINA cost on your *Adventure Sheet*, return to **34**.

265

You lift the lid of the chest and close your eyes as quickly as you can. But you have already seen the letter D written in gold dust on the bottom of the chest. Lose 4 STAMINA points. If you have seen all the letters D, E, A, T and H, turn to **148**. If you have not seen all of them, turn to **304**.

266

The tentacles carry the two main nerves of the Sand Snapper, which cannot function any longer. Its hideous maw falls open and you are able to withdraw your badly cut leg. Lose 4 STAMINA points and 1 SKILL point. After bandaging your leg with strips of torn shirt, you limp off south (turn to **106**).

267

You awake with a start when you hear a deep humming coming from the corridor on the other side of the golden rain. The sleep has refreshed you, and you jump up feeling alert. Add 2 STAMINA points. There is a door behind the drapes, but it is locked and there is no time to open it. If you wish to hide behind the drapes, turn to **44**. If you wish to confront whoever is coming into the chamber, turn to **227**.

268

Although light shines through the open door, you can see nothing beyond the doorway. If you can and wish to cast a Light spell, turn to **383**. If you wish to step slowly into total darkness, turn to **326**.

269

As the liquid washes over your wounds, they heal before your eyes. But although the magical healing properties of the herbal liquid are strong, its recuperative powers are quite weak. Thus your STAMINA is increased by only 4 points. Nevertheless, you are pleased to be healed, and walk back down the corridor feeling confident. Turn to **364**.

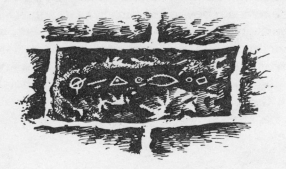

270

The Gnome shrieks in terror when his serpent pro-
tector is slain. In a frantic voice he begs you not to
harm him. If you talk to him, turn to **83**. If you slay
him, turn to **61**.

271

There is a solid oak door at the top of the steps. You
turn the handle and are surprised to find that it is
not locked. You are even more surprised that the
door opens out beyond the city wall into the Desert
of Skulls. The bright sunlight hurts your eyes after
the gloom of the dungeon catacombs. You look
down at the sand and see footsteps leading away
from the door around the city wall. If you wish to
follow the footsteps, turn to **394**. If you would rather
walk back down the steps and head the opposite
way along the corridor, turn to **358**.

272

On the third day you finally sight land, and the current carries you towards the shore. Fortunately, you are washed up on a sandy beach, but you realize that you have drifted a long way south. It is hot, and your mouth is parched. All you can see is sand, and the desert landscape stretches as far as the horizon. *Test your Luck*. If you are Lucky, turn to **78**. If you are Unlucky, turn to **352**.

273

The door opens into a narrow sloping corridor which leads into another chamber. The walls are covered with hieroglyphics, and there are three clay pots standing on top of a stone table. Will you:

Lift the lid of the white pot?	Turn to **14**
Lift the lid of the black pot?	Turn to **156**
Lift the lid of the red pot?	Turn to **183**
Walk through the chamber to the archway in the far wall?	Turn to **20**

274

Two figures come into sight – a chill runs down your spine. With armour hanging loosely on their yellow bones, two Skeleton Warriors walk jerkily towards you, armed with swords.

	SKILL	STAMINA
First SKELETON WARRIOR	7	5
Second SKELETON WARRIOR	6	6

Both Skeletons attack you at once. They will make a separate attack on you in each Attack Round, but you must choose which of the two you will fight each time. Attack your chosen Skeleton as in a normal battle. Against the other you will throw for your Attack Strength in the normal way, but you will not wound it if your Attack Strength is greater; you must just count this as though you have defended yourself against its blow. Of course, if its Attack Strength is greater, it will wound you. If you win, turn to **310**.

275

You become slightly delirious in the desert heat, because of mild sunstroke. Lose 1 SKILL point. Nevertheless, you press steadily on south (turn to **164**).

276

You place the key inside the lock and turn it to the right. The lock clicks open and you are able to push the door inwards. Turn to **88**.

277

Nothing happens when you put the ring on your finger, and you decide to leave it on. Will you:

Lift the lid of the black pot?	Turn to **156**
Lift the lid of the red pot?	Turn to **183**
Walk through the chamber to the archway in the far wall?	Turn to **20**

278

The captain laughs and says, 'Stranger, you are telling the truth, but I fear you have a lot of explaining to do.' That evening, over dinner, you tell the captain and his crew about your mission and its importance. Obviously concerned with the impending doom about to befall the good people of Allansia, the captain offers to sail south to the Desert of Skulls. Two days later the man-of-war drops anchor and you are rowed ashore to a white sandy beach. With your Provisions restored to provide for ten meals, courtesy of the ship's cook, you wave goodbye and set off on foot. All you can see is sand, and the desert landscape stretches as far as the horizon. If you wish to walk east inland, turn to **327**. If you would rather walk south along the coast, turn to **151**.

279

You raise the war-hammer into the air and bring it crashing down on top of the Dragon. It rebounds off it, leaving the artefact completely unmarked. You have chosen the wrong Dragon to destroy. You feel suddenly very weak as an unseen evil force tries to protect the artefact. Lose 1 SKILL point and 2 STAMINA points. Which Dragon will you now attempt to destroy?

The Bone Dragon?	Turn to 362
The Silver Dragon?	Turn to 231
The Crystal Dragon?	Turn to 9
The Gold Dragon?	Turn to 247

280

Despite the Phantom's powerful stare, you keep control of your mind. With its arms outstretched, the Phantom closes in to touch you, in order to intensify its power. If you wish to fight the Phantom with your sword, turn to 225. If you would rather rummage quickly through your backpack for an item to use against it, turn to 244.

281

You cup your hands together and say the words of the Create Water spell. Water immediately fills your hands, and you drink long and hard. Only when you separate your hands does the water stop flowing. Feeling refreshed, you set off in the direction of the noonday sun (turn to 116).

282

You swing your sword towards Leesha, but it meets an invisible barrier. Her sadistic laugh echoes around the temple and you find yourself riveted to the spot. Unable to move a muscle, you see a door open in the wall behind the couch and a man walk into the temple. His face is a manifestation of evil and the sickening truth dawns on you that it is Malbordus. His bony fingers search through your belongings, taking what Dragon artefacts you have. He then bows to Leesha and exits through the same door, leaving you to your fate. There is nothing you can do now to save the people of Allansia. Malbordus will fly back to Darkwood Forest with his Dragons, and chaos will consume the land. You have failed in your mission.

283

Inside the wooden box you find a mirror and a sealed clay pot. You place the mirror in your backpack and decide what to do with the clay pot. If you wish to break it open, turn to 50. If you would rather leave it inside the box, and continue your trek, turn to 70.

284

The Dark Disciples believe your story, but say that they cannot allow you to take the gift to Leesha herself. They say they will take it to her on your behalf. Deduct one item from your Equipment List. As they begin to argue about which of them should take the gift to Leesha, you slip past them and walk towards the archway in the wall behind the altar. Turn to 341.

285

Although the scrubland is quite barren, you are surprised to see a patch of ground which is totally black. There is a smell of decay in the air, which appears to be coming from the black patch. Holding your nose, you walk over to inspect the patch and see that there is a bronze medallion lying in its centre with the letter M etched deeply into it. Could the medallion have been dropped accidentally by Malbordus? If you wish to pick up the medallion, turn to 226. If you would rather leave it where it is lying and walk on south, turn to 159.

286

The chair starts to vibrate slightly and you get ready to jump off it. But you feel a tingling sensation run through your body, which is very soothing. After five minutes of this gentle vibration, you reluctantly leave the chair. The invigorating effect adds 4 points to your STAMINA. With bounding strides you set off once more. Turn to 202.

287

You prise open the chest and find a polished iron helmet inside. If you wish to place the helmet on your head, turn to 97. If you would rather leave it and walk south along the corridor, turn to 140.

288

A man's head suddenly appears from the pit, his face a manifestation of evil. The ground below him rises up slowly until his feet are level with the floor of the room. He walks slowly towards you, saying, 'Give me the Dragons I seek.' You shrink back, uncertain of what terrible powers Malbordus might possess. He suddenly claps his hands together and a deafening thunderbolt shatters the silence of the room. Cracks appear in the floor and walls, and the pain in your ears is unbearable. If you are wearing a copper ring, turn to 334. If you are not wearing a copper ring, turn to 351.

289

Although the heat is insufferable, your headscarf protects you from sunstroke, and you press resolutely on south (turn to 164).

290

You seize the silver rod and, to your immense relief, the ceiling stops its descent. You wonder how to open the door opposite the one through which you entered. If you have a crystal key or are able to cast an Open Door spell, turn to 178. If you do not possess a crystal key and are unable to cast the spell, turn to 366.

291

As you walk through the shadow cast by the huge idol, it suddenly starts to move. Its stone joints grind and creak as it steps off its pedestal. The Stone Golem lumbers towards you with its war-hammer raised.

STONE GOLEM   SKILL 8   STAMINA 12

If you manage to defeat the Golem, turn to **172**.

292

You manage to pull your hand out of the pot before the claws can dig into your skin. You slam the lid back on the pot, and decide what to do. Will you:

Lift the lid of the white pot?	Turn to **14**
Lift the lid of the red pot?	Turn to **183**
Walk through the chamber to the archway in the far wall?	Turn to **20**

293

The scene of the battle gradually fades from view as you drift away, clinging to the masthead. You drift for two days and become very weak. Roll two dice and deduct the total from your STAMINA. If you are still alive, turn to **272**.

294

The nearest Skeleton Man extends his free hand and tells you to give him the tooth. If you wish to give it to him, turn to **346**. If you decide not to trust the Skeleton Men and would rather fight them, turn to **211**.

295

As you reach up to prise the grille from the wall, you notice that it has been tampered with. Two of the vertical bars and the joining horizontal bar have been highlighted with white chalk to form a distinctive letter H in the centre of the grille. The Messenger of Death has struck. Lose 4 STAMINA points and 1 LUCK point. You reach up into the recess behind the grille, but find that it is merely an air-vent. Cursing your bad luck, you walk on. Turn to **157**.

296

If you wish to reply that you do like the artist's work, turn to **181**. If you wish to reply that you do not like it at all, turn to **105**.

297

You cup your hands together and say the words of the Create Water spell. Water suddenly fills your hands, and you gulp it down in long, delicious mouthfuls. The afternoon sun continues to beat down relentlessly, its intensity causing shimmering waves of heat to rise from the parched sand. When you have finally drunk your fill, you separate your hands to stop the flow of water and press on across the desert (turn to 24).

298

The door opens into a room which is completely empty. There is a mosaic floor which has an abstract pattern, except for the area in front of the door in the opposite wall, where there is the head of Medusa. On the door there is a small box with a slot on its top. You walk up to the door, turn the handle and find that it is unlocked. If you wish to put a Gold Piece into the box before stepping through the doorway, turn to 214. If you would rather walk through without making a donation, turn to 268.

299

The Eye Stinger floats over your thrusting sword and brushes your face with its deadly spines. All your muscles suddenly tighten as its petrifying poison races through your veins. Later that day the Serpent Guards will take you away to join the other gargoyles on top of the city walls. Your adventure ends here.

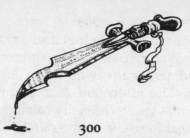

300

'Well done,' continues the talking head. 'You have answered correctly.' Red smoke starts to pour from its mouth and swirl around your face. When it finally drifts away, the bronze head is still and silent. You are left feeling powerful and as though destiny is with you. Add 2 SKILL points and 2 LUCK points. With renewed enthusiasm, you walk out of the room and up the corridor. Turn to **17**.

301

Yaztromo explains that his Jump spell will enable you to jump over walls or across pits at will. He tells you the incantation necessary to cast the spell and says that the energy required to use the spell drains 3 STAMINA points each time it is used. After noting down the spell and its STAMINA cost on your *Adventure Sheet*, return to **34**.

302

The carving is very intricate and must have taken months to complete. You look at the buildings and suddenly notice that there is a hairline crack running at roof-level. You find that one of the roofs lifts up and the inside of the building has been hollowed out. Your luck is in, for inside the building is a small Dragon carved out of ebony. Add 1 LUCK point for discovering a Dragon artefact. You smile to yourself and slip it into your pocket before opening the door in the wall opposite. Turn to 93.

303

Half an hour later, you see a low brown tent which you recognize as the type used by desert nomads. A horse is tethered to one of the tent-pegs. If you wish to make contact with the nomad, turn to 196. If you would rather head south to avoid the nomad, turn to 389.

304

You curse the Messenger of Death, but sense that you have survived its evil game. With a sudden rush of determination, you run through the doorway after Leesha. Turn to 137.

305

Up ahead in the sky, you see something flying towards you. As it gets closer, you see that it is a creature with the body of a large bird of prey, but the upper torso of a woman. It begins to emit a piercing shriek, which you instantly recognize. You frantically plug your ears with cloth that you rip from your shirt, so as not to hear the mesmerizing call of the dreaded Harpy. If you can and wish to cast a Magic Arrow spell, turn to **184**. Otherwise you must fight the Harpy with your sword (turn to **75**).

306

You roll the dying man over and see that he has not long to live. Being a valiant warrior, he wanted to keep fighting to the end. You ask him why he is here, for he clearly looks like an outsider. In an almost inaudible whisper he replies, 'The golden skeleton . . . it's here somewhere . . . beware the shadow of the stone . . .' Then he falls silent and still. You place his sword in his hand, as he would have wanted, and continue along the corridor. It soon turns right again and you reach an iron door in the right-hand wall. In the distance you can see glowing lights dancing about in the gloom of the corridor. If you wish to open the iron door, turn to **153**. If you wish to investigate the moving lights, turn to **339**.

307

The door opens and you walk into a room filled with treasure. There are chalices, statuettes, chests filled with gems, caskets and hundreds of fabulous artefacts. Will you:

Help yourself to some of the gems?	Turn to **143**
Take the golden skeleton statuette?	Turn to **386**
Open the golden casket?	Turn to **82**
Leave the room by the door opposite?	Turn to **3**

308

As the ship starts to sink, all the cannon crew run towards the wooden steps that lead to the upper deck. You are one of the first to reach the steps and manage to get on deck just as the ship goes underwater. If you wish to grab a piece of the masthead and drift away from the man-of-war, turn to **293**. If you wish to swim towards the man-of-war, turn to **230**.

309

As you sling your backpack off your shoulders, another bolt of light shoots out from the rod. *Test your Luck*. If you are Lucky, turn to **145**. If you are Unlucky, turn to **121**.

310

You take a shield from one of the broken Skeletons and sling it over your arm. Add 1 SKILL point. The corridor finally ends at a wooden door which is firmly locked. If you can and wish to cast an Open Door spell, turn to **114**. If you have an iron key, turn to **276**. If you have no means of opening the door, turn to **399**.

311

You draw your sword and try to help the eagle in its desperate fight. But the Pterodactyl stays out of reach and you are unable to influence the outcome of the bloody battle of beaks and talons. Resolve the battle between the eagle and the Pterodactyl.

	SKILL	STAMINA
GIANT EAGLE	6	11
PTERODACTYL	7	9

If the eagle wins the aerial battle, turn to **242**. If the Pterodactyl wins, turn to **48**.

312

With no defence against the relentless battering from the Wind Elemental, you are beaten to a bloody pulp. Your adventure ends here.

313

You suddenly remember that a single glance from the piercing eyes of the Basilisk is enough to kill you. If you possess a mirror, turn to **357**. If you do not possess a mirror and are able to cast a Fire spell, turn to **189**. If you are unable to do either, turn to **134**.

314

You push on the iron door and it swings slowly inwards. You enter a cold room with a high vaulted ceiling. The room is featureless, and Leesha is nowhere to be seen. There is, however, a circular pit in the middle of the room. Sensing that time is short, you decide to check your possessions. If you have collected five Dragon artefacts, turn to **35**. If you have not found all five of the Dragon artefacts, turn to **160**.

315

You soon arrive at a T-junction. Looking right you see that the floor is covered with broken glass, and so you turn left into the new corridor. Turn to **49**.

316

You soon discover that the smoke is rising from the burning roof of a wooden hut. Two Dark Elves in their familiar black, hooded cloaks are firing flaming arrows at the hut. Suddenly a man appears at the door, forced out by the choking smoke. Armed with a sword and a shield, you watch him run towards his attackers. Before you can help, he is cut down by two arrows. The Dark Elves step out from behind cover and walk towards their dead victim. If you wish to attack the Dark Elves, turn to 113. If you would rather not get involved and head south, turn to 285.

317

The Phantom snatches the charm out of the air and crushes it into dust. Laughing at your pathetic attempt to destroy it, the Phantom grabs your arm with its free hand and you are instantly paralysed. Lose 4 STAMINA points. By the time feeling has returned to your limbs, the Phantom is well out of sight. Walking stiffly along the tunnel, you continue your search. Turn to 190.

318

As soon as you touch the monkey's paw, its fingers twitch and with a will of its own, it tries to grasp your hand. *Test your Luck*. If you are Lucky, turn to 292. If you are Unlucky, turn to 222.

319

You toss the Pearl at the large eye of the vile creature, but it merely bounces off and falls down a crack in the stone floor. In haste, you draw your sword. Turn to **236**.

320

The corridor ends at a flight of steps. If you wish to climb up the steps, turn to **271**. If you would rather walk back and head the opposite way along the corridor, turn to **358**.

321

You tell the Gnome that you do not own a telescope. Disappointed by your reply, he rubs his chin and says, 'Well, you see, I really like brass, so if you have anything made of brass, I'll gladly give you a magical armband that will give strength to your sword-arm in battle.' If you own a brass handbell and wish to trade it, turn to **69**. Otherwise you will not be able to barter with the Gnome and will have to climb down the ladder and walk back down the corridor past the last junction. Turn to **262**.

322

After uttering the spell (deduct 2 STAMINA points), you hear the lock click open. Holding on to the hilt of your sword, you open the door. Turn to **98**.

323

You drop the burning medallion on to the sand and see a large and painful letter M branded on to the palm of your hand. Unfortunately it is your sword-hand. Lose 2 SKILL points and 1 STAMINA point. Realizing that Malbordus must be ahead of you, you continue south as quickly as possible (turn to 159).

324

The artefact looks harmless lying on the floor, but you suspect that destroying it will not be an easy matter. If you are carrying a war-hammer, turn to 279. If you do not have this weapon, turn to 193.

325

Luckily you find toe-holds and hand-holds which have been hacked out of the pit wall, and you are able to climb painfully out. Not daring to rest, you press on down the corridor. Turn to 152.

326

Your hands touch rough stone on either side of you, and you realize that you are in a corridor. Your heart thumps as you make your way slowly down the corridor. But what you are unable to see is a sharp blade which is set between the walls, less than a metre from the ground. It cuts painfully into your shin, and as you feel the blood start to run down your leg, you start to panic. Lose 2 STAMINA points and 1 LUCK point. Eager to escape from the black corridor, you run along it, bumping into a door at the far end. Turn to 79.

327

As you walk steadily east, you are suddenly aware of a buzzing sound overhead. You look up and see three giant wasp-like insects hovering above your head. Suddenly one of the three Needle Flies dives down at you. If you wish to cast a Magic Arrow spell, turn to **118**. If you wish to fight the giant insects with your sword, turn to **28**.

328

The man hears you close the door and advances towards you to attack you with his branding iron.

TORTURER   SKILL 8   STAMINA 8

If you win, turn to **141**.

329

Poking your head through the hole in the ceiling, you see a small, cluttered room lit by a single candle resting on top of a table. Crouched in a corner of the room is a sinewy little man wearing ragged sackcloth. On seeing you, he snatches a wooden pole off the floor. Will you:

Talk to him?	Turn to **83**
Attack him with your sword?	Turn to **240**
Climb down the ladder and walk back past the junction?	Turn to **262**

330

The corridor ends at a T-junction; patterned drapes hang down from ceiling to floor on the far wall. Will you:

Pull back the drapes?	Turn to 170
Turn left along the corridor?	Turn to 335
Turn right along the corridor?	Turn to 162

331

You run forward to stab the Night Horror with the long tooth, but it is broken into tiny pieces by another bolt from the rod. You have no choice but to attack it with your sword. Turn to 85.

332

The old man hobbles ahead of you along the street and stops in front of a dilapidated house. He knocks loudly on the door three times with his stick. Suddenly the door flies open and two rough-looking men run out brandishing cudgels. You hardly have time to draw your sword before being set upon by the robbers. Fight them one at a time.

	SKILL	STAMINA
First ROBBER	8	7
Second ROBBER	7	7

If you win, turn to 89.

333

As you walk along the corridor, you suddenly become aware of the sound of footsteps marching towards you. If you wish to see who is coming down the corridor, turn to **274**. If you would rather turn back and hurry down the corridor straight past the last junction, turn to **250**.

334

The ring you found in the pot is a ring of protection. The pain in your ears quickly fades away and you are able to draw your faithful sword to fight a last desperate battle. Turn to **380**.

335

The bare corridor turns sharply right. After ten metres you see an alcove in the left-hand wall. A trickle of water drips from a bronze cherub's mouth into a bowl at its feet. If you wish to drink the water, turn to **4**. If you would rather continue walking along the corridor, turn to **370**.

336

If you wish to cast an Open Door spell, turn to **369**. If you wish to hack the lock open with your sword, turn to **68**.

337

If the birds had been any lower in the sky, you would have recognized them as vultures. Waiting for another victim to fall dead by the side of the poisoned water-hole, they circle watchfully in the sky. Once again their patience has been rewarded.

338

Your sword-hand is badly burnt and some of your dexterity in combat will be lost. Lose 1 STAMINA point and 2 SKILL points. You withdraw your hand quickly and decide what to do next. Will you:

Take the golden skeleton statuette?	Turn to **386**
Open the golden casket?	Turn to **82**
Leave the room by the door opposite?	Turn to **3**

339

As you move closer to the glowing lights, you realize that they are starting to move towards you. Three giant bugs with wings buzz loudly and close in to attack. Fight the Giant Fireflies one at a time.

	SKILL	STAMINA
First GIANT FIREFLY	5	4
Second GIANT FIREFLY	5	5
Third GIANT FIREFLY	4	6

Each time a Firefly wins an Attack Round, roll one die. If the number rolled is 1, 2 or 3, the Firefly will discharge electricity and you will lose an additional 2 STAMINA points. If the number rolled is 4, 5 or 6, the Firefly will not discharge electricity. If you win, turn to **38**.

340

Running along the corridor, you see an iron grille high up in the right-hand wall. If you wish to prise it open with your sword, turn to **295**. If you would rather walk on, turn to **157**.

341

The archway has an elaborate surround of carved stone. You look through the archway into a corridor and see what looks like a shimmering gold curtain at the far end. Mounted along the walls are swords gripped by stone hands. Holding your sword tightly, you step warily along the corridor. As soon as you reach the first sword, its stone arm jerks into life and attacks you, while the other three cut through the air, awaiting their turn.

	SKILL	STAMINA
First SWORD	6	4
Second SWORD	6	4
Third SWORD	6	4
Fourth SWORD	6	4

If you win, turn to **191**.

342

Yaztromo explains that his Detect Trap spell will forewarn you of any dangerous trap which might be laid before you, although you will still have to overcome the problem using your own initiative. He tells you the incantation necessary to cast the spell and says that each time you use it, you will drain 2 STAMINA points of energy. After noting down the spell and its STAMINA cost on your *Adventure Sheet*, return to **34**.

343

There is a sudden blinding flash as the rod backfires and shoots out an arc of light into your stomach. Lose 2 SKILL points and 4 STAMINA points. If you survive the blast, turn to **169**.

344

The corridor turns right, and around the corner you see a man lying face down on the stone floor. He is wearing bloodstained armour, and his sword lies a metre away. He grunts on hearing your footsteps, and tries to reach for his sword. Will you:

Run him through with your sword?	Turn to **101**
Kick his sword away and try to talk to him?	Turn to **306**
Step over him and walk on?	Turn to **80**

345

You cup your hands together and chant the spell. Water fills your hands and you gulp it down. When you have drunk all you want, you separate your hands and press on south. Turn to **377**.

346

The Skeleton Man takes the tooth and suddenly hurls it to the floor, smashing it into tiny pieces. Their expressionless faces seem somehow relieved, and you wonder what mistake you have made. With their spears at the ready, they advance towards you.

	SKILL	STAMINA
First SKELETON MAN	9	6
Second SKELETON MAN	9	8

Fight them one at a time. If you win, turn to **96**.

347

The tunnel eventually comes to a dead end. A solitary candle burns in an alcove and you see something glistening behind it. If you wish to reach into the alcove, turn to **212**. If you would rather go back down the corridor and turn right along the other branch of the tunnel, turn to **59**.

348

You reach the bottom of the staircase and step warily along the floor with your arms stretched out in front of you. Suddenly you hear a plopping noise which sounds like a dollop of mud dropping on to the floor. *Test your Luck*. If you are Lucky, turn to **57**. If you are Unlucky, turn to **176**.

349

After untying the cord, you slowly pull open the cotton sack. Inside you find a glass ball, inside which a tiny man with pointed ears and wings, wearing a pea-green costume, is jumping up and down in a joyous frenzy. You cannot hear his voice through the glass, but you realize that the Sprite wants to escape. If you wish to release the Sprite, turn to **234**. If you would rather leave the Sprite in his glass prison and continue south, turn to **39**.

350

The Phantom cringes on seeing the silver and tries to run away. But your aim is true and the silver button finds its mark. The Phantom drops to the floor and within seconds is no more than dust spread among the folds of its cloak. Add 1 LUCK point. With renewed spirit, you set off down the tunnel. Turn to **190**.

351

You cover your ears, but you cannot stop the pain. You reel about, completely disorientated, and unable to keep your balance. Lose 3 SKILL points. Despite your disadvantage, you draw your faithful sword to fight a last desperate battle. Turn to **103**.

352

Walking along the beach, you find a cluster of palm trees, but no coconuts are growing on them. You look around and decide which way to head. If you wish to walk east inland, turn to **327**. If you would rather walk south along the coast, turn to **151**.

353

You follow the corridor until it turns sharply left. On turning the corner, you see that the floor is covered with broken glass. As you pick your way through the glass, a shadowy figure suddenly appears in the corridor ahead. You hear a shriek of laughter as a bottle is hurled at you. It shatters on the stone floor at your feet to reveal a piece of rolled-up parchment lying among the broken glass. If you wish to read what is on the parchment, turn to **256**. If you would rather chase after whoever threw the bottle at you, turn to **77**.

354

Although the golden rain feels wet on your skin, you remain completely dry. You step into a luxurious chamber whose walls are decorated with frescos and paintings. The floor is made of polished marble, and on it stand several low tables; cushions are scattered around the shining floor. A huge bare-chested man with a bald head, clad in baggy silk pants, is standing with his feet apart at the far end of the room. His hands are resting on the hilt of a curved sword. On seeing you, he immediately strides forward to attack. He is a Slave Guard of the outer temple.

SLAVE GUARD   SKILL 8   STAMINA 8

If you win, turn to **235**.

355

Without a supply of vital water, you grow steadily weaker; lose 1 SKILL point and 4 STAMINA points. You grit your teeth and stagger on in the direction of the noonday sun (turn to **116**).

356

Your frenzied dive through the doorway is not quick enough to prevent your lower torso from being crushed by the stone ceiling. There is a sickening crunch of bone as the ceiling meets the floor. Your adventure ends here.

357

With your eyes shut, you hold out the mirror at arm's length. You have discovered its only weakness: the Basilisk perishes by the strength of its own reflection. Hardly daring to look at the dead Basilisk, you hurry on south as fast as you can (turn to 108.

358

You come across a bowl on a marble column. The bowl is filled with grapes which look fresh and juicy. If you wish to eat the grapes, turn to 112. If you would rather continue without eating, turn to 237.

359

You run away from the beach as fast as you can, but are unable to escape from the Shell Monster. You fall over in the sand and wave after wave of flying shells lash your body. Slowly you lose consciousness and your adventure ends on the edge of the Desert of Skulls.

360

The chair suddenly heats up and you find yourself sitting on stone which feels near-molten in temperature. Roll one die and deduct the total from your STAMINA. If you are still alive, you leap out of the chair and stagger on down the corridor. Turn to 202.

361

As soon as you reveal the Onyx Egg, the Eye Stinger becomes motionless and closes its central eye. You seize your opportunity and run past the Eye Stinger, holding up the Onyx Egg to protect you. Turn to 340.

362

You raise the war-hammer into the air and bring it crashing down on top of the Bone Dragon. The artefact splinters into tiny fragments and you allow yourself a smile of satisfaction. You raise the war-hammer a second time, but suddenly hear the sound of thunder coming from the depths of the pit. Turn to 288.

363

You draw your sword and try to cut down the eagle's fearsome attacker. But the Pterodactyl stays out of your reach and you are unable to help in the battle between the two flying creatures. Resolve the battle between the eagle and the Pterodactyl.

	SKILL	STAMINA
GIANT EAGLE	6	11
PTERODACTYL	8	9

If the eagle wins the aerial battle, turn to 242. If the Pterodactyl wins, turn to 48.

364

Passing by the Sphinx chair and the tapestries, you walk straight on past the junction in the corridor to look at the murals. Turn to 161.

365

You enter a dust-filled room, which has dried blood smeared all over its walls. There is a bucket hanging down from the ceiling on a rope just above your head. In the wall opposite you there is another door, and in the wall to the left there is a low arch from which you can hear the sound of scratching. A huge, black insect's head suddenly appears out of the dark hole, followed by a long and many-legged body. The Giant Centipede rushes from its lair to bite you.

GIANT CENTIPEDE   SKILL 9   STAMINA 7

If you win, turn to **393**.

366

You examine the silver rod, hoping to find out how it can be activated to fire a bolt of light. You notice two tiny raised circles on the surface of the rod, and realize that one must be its firing-button. You point the rod at the door and decide which circle to press. If you press the circle on the left of the rod, turn to **343**. If you press the circle on the right, turn to **167**.

367

Yaztromo explains that his Create Water spell will fill your hands with drinking water each time you cup them together. He tells you the incantation necessary to cast the spell and says that, curiously, this spell requires no energy at all to cast. After noting down the spell on your *Adventure Sheet*, return to **34**.

368

The crossbow bolt sinks deep into your throat. You gasp for air, but your frantic efforts are useless. Your adventure ends here.

369

You utter the words of the spell (reducing your STAMINA by 2 points), but nothing happens. Unknown to you, the golden rain has drained away all your magic powers. Lose 1 LUCK point. You have no choice but to hack the lock open with your sword. Turn to **68**.

370

The corridor turns sharply to the right again and soon you arrive at another T-junction. The corridor is bare and uninteresting straight ahead, so you decide to turn left. Turn to **46**.

371

You utter the words of the spell (lose 1 STAMINA point), but nothing happens. Unknown to you, the golden rain has drained away all your magical powers. The nearest Skeleton Man lunges at you with his spear and you have no option but to fight. Turn to **211**.

372

You cup your hands together and chant the Create Water spell. Water suddenly fills your hands and you gulp it down in long, delicious mouthfuls. The afternoon sun continues to beat relentlessly down, its intensity causing shimmering waves of heat to rise from the parched sand. You separate your hands to halt the flow of water, and you press on across the desert (turn to 303).

373
The serpent's poison is deadly. It only takes one bite to end your life. Your eyes close for the last time as the serpent stiffens to become a snake staff again.

374
The chanting seems to grow louder, and you cannot stop yourself from slowly walking towards the altar. You lie down on the cool marble top and are aware of the Dark Disciples surrounding you. You hear one of them say that it is midnight and then you are dimly aware of another pulling a dagger from his belt. Your last vision is of the dagger plunging into your chest. Your adventure ends here.

375
As you pull away the rock, a scorpion runs out from the shadow of its dark crevice and stings you on the back on the hand. Lose 4 STAMINA points. If you are still alive, turn to 155.

376

The corridor bends to the right, and you follow it round until you arrive outside a closed door. You can hear agonized cries and a sadistic chuckle coming from inside the room. If you wish to turn the handle and push the door open, turn to 206. If you would rather ignore the cries and keep on walking, turn to 66.

377

Walking steadily south, you are unaware of the unseen danger in front of you. Your right foot sinks into the sand and you feel a sharp pain as something begins to tear at the flesh on your leg. You stab your sword into the sand as a Sand Snapper tries to overcome you. It shudders, and the sand is shaken off its brown body to reveal its gaping maw, crammed with cutting teeth. It is impossible to penetrate the thick scales covering its hide. Some of the scales are suddenly pushed apart by two long tentacles which try to grab you and pull you into the Sand Snapper's mouth. Ignoring the pain in your leg, you begin to hack at the tough tentacles.

	SKILL	STAMINA
First TENTACLE	7	7
Second TENTACLE	7	7

If either of the two tentacles wins two consecutive Attack Rounds during the combat, turn to 149. If you manage to cut off both tentacles, turn to 266.

378

You peer into the gloom of the Death Dog's lair and see that a dark tunnel stretches into the distance. If you wish to crawl down the tunnel, turn to 95. If you would rather leave the room and continue walking up the corridor, turn to 344.

379

Looking up, you see a road sign indicating that you are in Clog Street. You walk down it all the way until it ends at a T-junction where it meets Harbour Street, which runs parallel to the shore. You look out to sea and watch the setting sun sink slowly beneath the horizon. Darkness envelops you and you wonder where to go next. At the end of the street to your left there are lights shining in windows, and you can just hear the sound of singing and laughter. You decide to head towards the lights and soon find yourself outside the Black Lobster tavern. You walk through the doorway into a smoke-filled room where seedy-looking characters sit at crowded tables, laughing, joking and singing. You walk straight up to the barman and ask if he has a room for rent. Luckily there is one available. You pay him 1 Gold Piece for the room and ask if he knows of any ships which may be sailing south the next morning. 'I might do,' he replies somewhat cagily, 'but information does not come free in Port Blacksand. Another Gold Piece and I'll introduce you to the ship's mate.' Once again you reach into your pocket and pay the barman. He leads you over to one of the booths along the far wall of the tavern and points out a man with a silk scarf tied over his bald head, and an ugly scar running down from his left ear to the middle of his chin. 'Gargo is his name,' says the barman. You sit down next to Gargo, introduce yourself and ask if you can buy your passage south. 'Ten Gold Pieces, and you'll have to work for your food,' comes the curt reply. Gargo does not look like a man to bargain with, so you agree to his price and pay. 'We set sail one hour after sunrise. The name of the ship is the *Belladonna* and you'll find her at the end of the jetty leading down from the tavern. I'll see you in the morning; I'm going back to the ship now,' says Gargo. You decide not to get involved with any of the tavern's characters, but to retire to your room. You stand up and walk towards the stairs, but a large man carrying three flasks of ale bumps into you, spilling the drinks on the floor. If you wish to offer to buy him more ale, turn to **124**. If you would rather tell him not to be so clumsy, turn to **203**.

380

Malbordus realizes that you are invulnerable to his magic powers and draws his cursed sword to attack you.

MALBORDUS   SKILL 10   STAMINA 18

If you win, turn to **400**.

381

You walk under the raised war-hammer of the idol towards the tunnel entrance (turn to **74**).

382

The door is firmly shut and will not open. If you can and wish to cast an Open Door spell, turn to **248**. If you are unable to or do not wish to cast this spell, turn to **210**.

383

Once you have uttered the words of the spell (deduct 2 STAMINA points), the corridor beyond the doorway is suddenly illuminated by bright light. But you have fallen into the hands of the Messenger of Death. A large letter A is painted on the door at the end of the corridor and you cannot avoid seeing it. Lose 4 STAMINA points as a result of the shock. The only consolation you have is that you see a blade which is set between the walls at knee height, and you are able to step over it without injury. Cursing your bad luck, you open the door at the end of the corridor. Turn to **79**.

384

You are now wearing an Armband of Strength. Add 1 SKILL point. You climb back down the ladder and walk back past the last junction. Turn to **262**.

385

The sand-storm takes a long time to die down and you lose a great deal of strength trying to protect yourself. Lose 1 SKILL point. Eventually the wind dies away. You brush yourself down and press on east (turn to **26**).

386

The statuette is heavy in your hand and is worth an unbelievable fortune. If you succeed in your mission, you will have been more than amply rewarded. Add 1 LUCK point. You place the statuette in your backpack and decide what to do next. Will you:

Help yourelf to some of the gems?	Turn to 143
Open the golden casket?	Turn to 82
Leave the room by the door opposite?	Turn to 3

387

Looking for a likely object with which to defeat the Eye Stinger, you must make a quick decision. Will you take:

A Mirror?	Turn to 65
A Pearl?	Turn to 319
An Onyx Egg?	Turn to 361
None of these?	Turn to 200

388

Sensing sudden danger, you utter the words of the spell (deduct 2 STAMINA points). A magical aura illuminates a crossbow that is mounted on the wall and a tripwire which is laid two metres in front of it. You climb over the wire without triggering it, and squeeze past the crossbow. The tunnel finally opens out into a dusty room lit by torches set in the wall. Turn to 43.

389

Not long after the tent is out of sight, you begin to feel a slight tremor in the ground beneath your feet. Suddenly the sand starts to shift before you. It rises into the air and then falls down in a great cascade to expose the long body of a huge worm. You realize with horror that a Giant Sandworm is about to engulf you with its spiked oval mouth. It is at least twenty metres long and you must fight it.

GIANT SANDWORM   SKILL 10   STAMINA 20

If you win, turn to 18.

390

As the Night Horror drops to the ground, it releases its grip on the silver rod. Suddenly there is a grating noise above you. Out of the hands of its owner, the rod has mysteriously triggered a mechanism in the stone ceiling, which is lowering down towards you. You frantically run to open one of the doors, but both are firmly locked by some powerful magic, and cannot be opened even by Yaztromo's spell. Will you:

Pick up the silver rod?	Turn to 290
Try a crystal key in the door (if you have one)?	Turn to 150
Try to burn a hole in the door with a Fire spell (if you are able)?	Turn to 239

391

Yaztromo explains that his Read Symbols spell will allow the user to read any runes or magic symbols. He tells you the incantation necessary to cast the spell and says that virtually no energy is required to cast it; only 1 STAMINA point is lost each time it is used. Return to **34** after writing down the spell and its STAMINA cost on your *Adventure Sheet*.

392

Not wishing to be a sacrificial victim, you concentrate on trying to blot out the chanting voices from your mind. Roll two dice. If the total is the same as or less than your SKILL, turn to **174**. If the total is greater than your SKILL, turn to **374**.

393

If you wish to cut down the bucket from the ceiling, turn to **60**. If you would rather open the iron door in the far wall, turn to **21**.

394

The door slams shut behind you and you find that it is firmly locked. You follow the footsteps around the city wall for about fifteen minutes until you find the man who made them. He is lying face down in the sand and appears to have been dead for at least a day. He looks like a servant and is certainly not Malbordus. There is nothing on the man which can help you, and so you run back to the oak door. Because you have passed through the golden rain, even your magic is useless against it, so you have to try to open it by hacking furiously with your sword. Suddenly a shadow passes overhead. You look up to see what caused it. Riding through the sky on the back of a huge, black Dragon is the man you came to defeat – Malbordus. The Dragon roars and you can just make out the wicked laugh of Malbordus. The Dragon flies off north and there is nothing you can do to stop it. Malbordus will lead his hordes of chaos across Allansia, and the world will fall under a dark shadow. You have failed in your mission.

395

It is so cold that you are hardly able to sleep at all during the night. Lose 3 STAMINA points. You are wide awake and thankful when the dawn sun rises over the horizon to heat up the desert air. As soon as it is light enough to see where you are walking, you continue your trek to the south (turn to **72**).

396

As you stab into the water, your bracelet is briefly submerged. The tentacled monster is immediately repelled by it and swims silently away to the deepest part of its pool. You seize your chance, climb up on to the ledge and escape down the tunnel. Turn to **91**.

397

Stairs lead down from the trapdoor into the g.
below. There is a strong, musty smell rising ou.
the gloom and the draught is cool on your face. Yo
walk down the rough staircase until you can see no
further. Will you:

Cast a Light spell? (if you are able to)?	Turn to 224
Walk further down into the gloom?	Turn to 348
Climb back up the steps and open the other door?	Turn to 307

398

In the middle of the night you are woken by the
sound of heavy footsteps stumping along the
ground. The moon is almost full and gives off
enough light for you to see a large shape looming
towards you. Grabbing your sword, you stand to
defend yourself against the Cave Troll who has
discovered you during its nocturnal hunt.

CAVE TROLL   SKILL 8   STAMINA 9

If you win, you try to settle down again, but toss and
turn for the rest of the night. In the morning, you set
off again. Turn to 305.

399

Unable to open the door, you turn around and walk
back down the corridor and past the last junction.
Turn to 250.

 _ordus is killed and the remaining Dragon arte-
_ts lie waiting to be destroyed. You bring the
_var-hammer crashing down on them time and time
again, so that no man or being might ever again
have the opportunity of using their power. In time
the Dark Elves of Darkwood Forest will learn of their
leader's defeat and will shrink back into the shadows of the forest. Your ordeal inside the Temple of
Terror has saved Allansia. You will now be able to
journey proudly back to Stonebridge and return the
war-hammer to King Gillibran. No doubt Yaztromo
will teach you some more of his magic, and perhaps
you will have the chance to spend some of the riches
you have found.